Giovanni's Obsession

Marissa Ann

Chapter 1
Giovanni

Walking into the cafe, I take a seat in the back, facing the door. It's the best way to not be caught unaware.

I'm only in town to gather Intel on a certain congressman for my employers. It seems he made them some promises that they intend for him to keep. No matter the cost.

"Can I take your order?" I turn to the voice and see the most beautiful woman I've ever seen. My eyes rake over her slowly.

"Coffee. Black." I murmur, not taking my eyes off of her even as she walks away.

What the fuck is wrong with me? I've seen beautiful women before.

Putting it out of my mind, I pull out my phone to send in an update, not bothering to look up when the waitress brings my coffee, setting it in front of me.

Her sweet smelling perfume seems to linger in the air around me. Looking up, I watch as she moves around from table to table taking orders.

She smiles at everyone politely but I notice it never reaches her eyes. No one else seems to notice the emptiness behind those dark eyes.

My phone pings telling me that the congressman is on the move. I toss a twenty on the table and head for the door.

Looking back one last time through the window, I catch sight of the waitress picking up the money with a smile that this time reaches her eyes.

Something jolts inside of me at the sight. I zero in on her name tag. Raven. The name seems to fit her perfectly.

Deciding right then, that I'll come back later to eat again even though as a rule I never return to the same place in such a short amount of time.

It's how I manage to stay under the radar. To not get caught. I'm not a good man by society's standards. I do the jobs that keep others' hands clean.

There is not a single government on this planet that is not bought and paid for in blood. If I'm ever caught, the government I work for would deny ever knowing me.

Following the tracker on my phone to a warehouse, I sneak in through a window, moving silently towards the voices that I hear in a heated discussion.

Getting into position so that I can listen in, I set up my enhanced recording device to pick up everything they say.

By the end of the impromptu meeting, I'm sure that I have more than enough for my employer to get what he wants from the congressman.

Three days later, I still haven't left town. Something about the little Raven at the cafe keeps drawing me back.

I've pretty much eaten every meal there. The truly crazy part? The woman never seems to be off work. I thought places like this did shifts that were split between all the employees yet she's here through every one of them, working the tables and sometimes helping out in the kitchen.

She's tried to engage in conversation with me on several occasions but I never answer with more than a yes or no.

While I've been studying her, I've noticed that she's started studying me. It's almost like she's not sure if she should run.

She's gotten more nervous around me as the days have passed. She spilled my coffee when filling my cup a few minutes ago.

I want to ask her what has her wound so tight that she looks ready to break but I keep my silence.

She's become an obsession that I don't need. I've already been called in for another job that I need to get to but I've put them off for now.

"I have to take the garbage out back. We'll be closing soon. Will you be okay out here by yourself for a few minutes?" I hear Raven's sweet voice ask from the counter.

Looking up into her eyes, she gets a deer in headlights look on her face. So, she feels something too? That's interesting.

"Yes. I'm going to finish my coffee." I say.

She stands there until I look away, breaking our connection. The small smile on my mouth feels foreign but I think I like it.

Raven

My heart races as I lean against the kitchen sink trying to catch my breath as if I've been running. Which is funny, because I have been running in a way.

That man just makes my nerves stand at attention for some reason. When he first started coming in for every single meal, I got nervous that they had found me again.

I'd rather die than to go back to a life where I would be expected to spread my legs for that sick fuck to plant his demon seed.

I got lucky that one of my dad's bodyguards made it out of the fire and got to me in time to save me at the cost of his own life. Now, I'm truly alone in the world. I only have myself to get me out of any danger.

I have to keep my eyes open at all times for the first sign that they have found me. It's best to not stay in one place too long. I've already been here longer than I wanted to be.

The boss man will pay my wages in two more days. I'll pack now and leave as soon as I get my money.

There has to be somewhere I can go and never be found. I'm so tired of running.

Throwing the trash in the dumpster, I go back through the back door making sure to lock it behind me.

I was so distracted; I didn't realize I walked out there without looking around first. Fuck! I'm slacking! It's definitely time to leave.

Walking back into the cafe I hear the handsome man at the counter waiting to pay his bill. He's the last customer of the night.

I've gotten used to him staying literally until I lock the doors. I'm not sure where he goes as I'm locking up but by the time I turn around he's nowhere to be seen. Almost like a ghost disappearing into thin air.

"Keep the change Raven." His deep accented voice says as he lays a twenty on the counter.

"Well, that's not fair." I say.

"What?" He stops to ask. I really expected him to do like any other time that I've tried to talk to him.

"You know my name but I don't know yours. I think that's not really fair considering you give me a nineteen dollar tip every single time you come in here." I look him straight in the eye and hold my breath waiting for him to say something else.

"Gio." He says.

"Joe? Your name is Joe?" That name just doesn't go with this man.

"No. Gio. It's short for Giovanni." He answers, holding the door open for me as we walk out, turning off the lights.

—

"It's really nice to meet you Gio. Did you just move here?" I ask, concentrating on locking the doors.

When he doesn't answer, I turn around and see that yet again he is gone. Like a vision that was never really there.

Shrugging my shoulders, I take off at a brisk walk towards my apartment. It's time to start packing.

Giovanni

I follow Raven from the shadows towards her apartment building. Last night was the first night I've ever done so. I spent the night on the fire escape under her bedroom window.

I honestly don't understand this obsessive need to be close to her. It's not like me at all. I'd text my brother about it but I don't want to disturb him on whatever mission he is currently on.

He'd probably say that I've slid the rest of the way onto the crazy train and that I should retire from this life.

I watch as she lets herself into her apartment before making my way to the side alley and up the fire escape to watch her from the window.

She flits from room to room, shoving clothes into bags and I briefly wonder if she's so untidy that she's got that much laundry to do. I realize it's not laundry when she begins pulling clothes from the drawers and closet.

"Where are you going little bird?" I whisper out loud.

Hearing a noise from down below, I lean over the rail silently to take a look. I can't make out the guy's features but there's definitely someone down there peeping into windows.

Moving to go back down, I step the wrong way with my boot making a small sound that must scare the fucker as he takes off running back down the alley.

Thinking he was probably just some homeless guy looking for trash, I look back through the window searching for Raven.

She must have gotten a shower because she walks into her bedroom in nothing but a towel with her hair all wet.

My body immediately takes notice. She's flawless with dark skin that makes my mouth water.

My eyes are riveted as she sits down on the edge of the bed, letting the towel drop to the floor. I know I should look away but I can't seem to help myself where she's concerned.

Hell, look at where I'm currently at instead of on my next mission where I'm supposed to be.

Watching her rub lotion down each leg, across her torso and her arms, my cock is rock hard, throbbing with a need like I've never felt before.

As I watch, the look on her face changes and I hold my breath as her hand slowly glides between her breasts, straight to her clit.

When her finger makes contact, her legs spread wider and she throws her head back.

I watch in fascination waiting for the moment she hits her peak. Her finger rubs faster and harder with each passing minute.

I can't keep myself from reaching down and squeezing my own cock, trying to relieve the pressure that's building from watching her get herself off.

Too soon, I see her mouth open on a scream that is muffled from the closed window. She lays on the bed, not moving for several long minutes before climbing further into the bed and pulling the covers over her.

She reaches to the lamp on the side table, cutting it off. Plunging the room into darkness like a T.V. being cut off.

I'm left on the fire escape, rock hard and breathing heavy. Wanting nothing more than to climb through the window, climb under those blankets and lick her dry.

That was the hottest thing I've ever witnessed in my entire life.

I'm entirely too obsessed with this woman. I'll give myself tomorrow but after that, I need to leave. Get back to my normal life.

Resolving to do just that, I silently climb down the fire escape. Giving one last look up to her window, I slip out into the darkness keeping to the shadows.

Raven

A noise wakes me in the early morning hours and I hold my breath to listen closely to see if I can figure out what it is.

Hearing it again, I realize it's just the stray cat I sometimes feed on the fire escape as it makes a pretty big meow at my window.

Getting up, I open the window and let her inside. She knows exactly where the food dish is at.

Petting her soft fur for a minute, I wonder about taking her with me although I'm not sure it's a good idea. It's hard enough running on my own. It'll be even harder with a pet.

"I could get you a pet crate from the store." I whisper to her as she purrs in my hand. "I'll take that as a yes." I smile.

Getting back up off the floor, I get back into bed to get some more sleep. Today is going to be a long day getting everything ready to go.

Walking into the cafe several hours later, I immediately notice Gio sitting in the back where he's always at.

I've wondered over the past week if the man is jobless since he seems to be here all day everyday.

His eyes look up in my direction and I quickly look away, going straight to the back to put my apron on.

The hours fly by instead of dragging because we were more busy than usual. There must be a convention going on in the hotel down the street.

"Hey Raven, Sal can cover the rest of the night. I have your paycheck ready on my desk." Bobby says from the door to the kitchen. "Can you take the garbage out on your way?"

"No problem. Thanks Bobby." I say with a smile.

"You come back to town, you know where there's a job waiting for you." He smiles back with a nod before disappearing into the kitchen again.

As I pass Gio's table, his voice stops me.

"Not working until close tonight?" He murmurs.

"No. This is actually my last night." I answer.

He just stares back, not saying anything and I continue to the office to get my check. I'll grab the garbage and leave out the back way.

Looking back, Gio's eyes are still on me.

"It was nice meeting you."

He just nods back and I disappear through the door.

Giovanni

Not much shocks me but the revelation that it was her last night at the cafe did. Did she find another job?

I already know the answer to that. I heard her boss say if she ever came back to town again she would have a job. That means she's leaving town.

Last night when I thought she was packing, I was right. But where she's going and why is a question I have this need to know.

After waiting fifteen minutes for her to come back, I realize she must have left out through the back when she took the garbage out.

Getting up, I throw down some money to cover my tab and walk out. I'll head to her apartment and try to track her without being seen. I can't let her just walk away without knowing where she's going.

As I walk past the alley, I hear a scuffle and a moan that sounds feminine. Knowing it's the same alley way that Raven would have been in, I stick to the shadows making my way towards the sounds.

"Hold her down!" I hear from the other end. "I'm about to get a piece of this bitch before we have to haul her ass back to Miami."

My eyes adjust to the darkness, taking in the scene. There on the ground is Raven. Either they knocked her out or she fainted. Probably both considering the way her face currently looks like it took way more than one hit.

Looking over the two fucks that look to be getting ready to stick their dick somewhere it should never be allowed, I notice they both have busted lips. Hopefully those shots came from Raven.

Before either can put their hands on her again, I lift my gun from inside my jacket, popping stupid fuck number one who thought he could take her, in the head. The silencer barely makes a sound.

As he falls to the ground, stupid fuck number two, trips over his feet trying to get away. When his hand lifts to the gun in his pants, I shoot out his right knee and he falls. Howling in pain.

"Don't reach for it again." I murmur, walking over to check Raven's pulse since she has yet to move.

Verifying that she's still breathing, I walk over to stupid fuck number two, grabbing his small gun, emptying it of bullets. Pathetic.

Pointing my gun at him, he stares back with huge eyes.

"You don't know what you're doing man." He says.

"Hmm. Why don't you start by telling me why you two were beating on this woman?" I simply wait for him to answer.

—

When he remains quiet, I reach over with my hand, squeezing the area where I shot him in the knee. He screams loudly. I just hope I can get the answers I need before someone else decides to investigate the noise from him screaming.

"Okay!" He screams, grabbing his leg.

Letting go, I back off just a little.

"Better talk quickly." I grin; waving my gun in his face to be sure I still have his full attention.

Out of the corner of my eye, I see Raven beginning to stir.

"My boss wants her back. She's his property." He says through gritted teeth.

"Last I checked you couldn't own people." He laughs at my statement.

"She definitely belongs to him. She's wearing his mark." He smiles as if he knows something that I don't, which pisses me off because he most likely does.

I hit him across the temple to make myself feel better especially when I notice that it busted his eye.

"Who exactly is your boss?" I ask quickly, wanting to be done and to get Raven somewhere I can check her injuries.

He spits towards me, "I'm not telling you shit! You're just going to kill me anyway."

Standing up, I look him right in the eye, "You're right. I'll get the information from her."

I raise my gun and squeeze the trigger. Now, how exactly am I going to get her out of here without drawing attention to the fact I'm carrying a very battered woman on my shoulder?

Chapter 2
Raven

The pain is what I feel first before I can even try to open my eyes. Neither of which are open enough to see where I'm at or how badly I've been hurt.

I do remember what happened though. Scotty's thugs found me. I waited too long. Trying to reach out with my hand, hoping to get a clue where I'm at, I stiffen the second I feel someone stop me from doing so.

"It's okay. You're safe. You are badly hurt and shouldn't move." I hear whispered from right beside me.

I can't tell who it is but the voice sounds vaguely familiar. It's certainly not the assholes that did this to me.

Someone must have scared them off before they could take me away. At least that's what I hope and that this person, whoever they are, does not plan to do the same.

I'll never go back, even if that means taking my own life. I've seen what he does to the women he claims to own. By the time he's finished with them, they all wish for death.

"Who…" I try to ask but my throat is too scratchy.

Feeling a straw at my lips, I eagerly sip at it, feeling thirstier than I've ever been.

"Don't drink too quickly. You should rest." When I feel the bed move like he stood up, I quickly grab hold of whatever I can. I know that it's stupid but for now he's being nice. I don't want him to leave me alone.

"I promise not to go far, little bird." Patting my hand, he lays it back onto the bed. "Rest. I'll be here when you wake up again. I promise." The more he talks to me; I realize I recognize that accent.

"Gio?" I whisper softly.

"Yes little bird. Now go to sleep." I feel his hand gently touch my cheek at the same time a tear falls from my eye.

For now I'm safe. And with that realization, I drift off to sleep.

Giovanni

I wait until she's fully asleep before I go into the other room to put on a pot of coffee. I'll need to stay up to watch her for a while longer although it's safe to say she'll fully recover.

Having retrieved her purse from the alley last night, I've already gone through the entire contents only to discover there's not a single thing inside of it to identify who she is.

Yes, I know she goes by Raven but what's her last name? Maybe Raven isn't her name at all.

She's important enough to someone that he'd send his minions to retrieve her and not give a damn in what condition she is returned.

Finding out who she is will be tricky. Thankfully I have contacts that have access to all government records and technology. Which includes the crazy facial recognition software the government secretly uses as well as fingerprint technology.

Since there is not a single picture of her in her purse and she doesn't seem to own a cell phone, I'll need to take my chances with her fingerprints which I already lifted from her before she woke up.

I would rather know who my enemy is before he ever knows about me. It's easier to kill your prey when they never realize they are being hunted.

I'll need to find a better place for us to go until I can figure out my plan. I don't like leaving things to chance. Staying here leaves the chance that the "boss" knew where his dogs were and just might send more guys to find out why they've not checked in.

We need to be long gone from here by then. Hopefully I can move her without causing too much more pain than what she is currently feeling just from laying on the bed.

Picking up the phone, I dial my brother's number. He has other connections that just might come in handy.

Raven

I drift in and out of consciousness without any sense of time passing. It feels as though only a few hours have passed.

At one point of wakefulness, I realize that there's an I.V. in my arm although I have no recollection of when Gio even put it there.

Considering that I hate needles, it's a damn good thing I was still passed out when he did it.

"Are you awake, little bird?" I hear his voice from the door.

Barely opening my eyes, I notice that I can see him slightly better than I could have before.

"Yes." I croak.

He walks further into the room, grabbing a water bottle with a straw and holding it up to my mouth letting me drink.

"Thank you." I whisper, he only nods back.

Looking around the space I'm currently occupying, I guess it to be a small apartment. Although it looks worse for wear, it's really clean and the sheets smell new.

"Where are we?" I ask.

"It's a small apartment complex that rents by the week." He answers, offering me some more water which I take gratefully.

"How long have I been asleep?" I ask, figuring it to only have been a few hours. My body is still hurting all over.

"You've been in and out for three days." His admission has my eyes widening so fast that it sends a sharp pain through my entire head and I groan.

"Head hurt?" I just nod my answer. He looks down at his watch, "It's time again for your pain meds anyway. The others are wearing off. I've been giving you morphine through your I.V. but do you think aspirin will cover it?"

I'm shocked yet again by what he says. Just who is this guy?

"Who are you?" I ask, needing to know.

"Giovanni. We've already met, remember? At the cafe?" He smiles slightly.

Rolling my eyes as best I can, I say, "That's not what I meant."

"I know what you meant." He sighs. "Can we save that conversation for later?" He asks.

Looking at him closely, I wonder for only a few minutes if I should be afraid of whom he really is.

This mysterious man that showed up out of nowhere and saved my life. I shake those thoughts quickly just from the look in his eyes. He has kind eyes, although he tries to hide it.

"Okay." I answer simply. "We'll talk about it later."

"Good. Now, do you think you can manage to eat a little something? I made some soup." He smiles as my stomach rumbles loudly right then.

"I think that's a yes." I whisper.

He nods once and leaves out the bedroom door. He doesn't close the door for which I am grateful.

Closed doors make me feel as though I am locked away.

I push myself up higher onto the bed, propping myself up with my pillows so that I can look around a bit more.

Thinking about how long I've been here, those assholes have had enough time to have contacted Scotty to let him know everything.

He'll most likely send even more men to help them track us down faster since he knows what city I've been hiding out in.

For all I know, he already has men here. He has contacts all over because of the business he's in. Gio and I will need to leave as soon as we can to get a head start.

My only hope is that he'll continue helping me, at least until I can find somewhere new to stay for a while undetected.

Giovanni

After helping Raven eat her soup, I sit with her long enough for her to fall back to sleep before leaving the room.

Sitting down at the kitchen table I open up the files that my contact sent to me on what he could find on Raven.

She was born to what appears to be a middle class family who seem to come into some money quite a few years back although there's no record of where it came from.

Her father seems to have ties to the Mendez family down in Miami Florida. They're mixed up in not only drugs but trafficking as well as murder although the FBI has been unable to make any charges stick.

There's not much I've not seen in this life that I've chosen to live. I've killed in my line of work, never blinking an eye and certainly not losing any sleep.

There's one thing though that I will not do. That is, to hurt a woman or child.

Don't get me wrong, I've probably met quite a few women that needed killing over the years but I've never done so.

My brother is the same as me. We have this code that we never break, no matter the circumstances. No women. No children.

The pictures of some of the crime scenes that the FBI have collected over the last three years, tells me that these people have no code.

They live only for the money. And there's plenty of that when you deal in trafficking women and children.

Looking back towards the bedroom, I'm filled with questions as to how mixed up with all of this she is.

Some of the pictures that are in the file makes it seem as though she had a romantic relationship with Mateo "Scotty" Mendez.

Is it possible she knew what was going on? That it was money from the sale of little kids that paid for her expensive dinners?

She did leave though. She's been running. For quite a while from what I've gathered. No, she's not involved.

I think she does know now though and it's possibly the reason she started running. She's been lucky so far that they've only just managed to catch up with her.

She doesn't need to worry any more though. I plan to put these fuckers in the ground. Sick fucks like these have no business being above ground.

First things first though. My brother is expecting us in Montana. His wife has a piece of land up on the mountain that has an old shack structure on it that does have a wood burning stove we can use to cook or stay warm.

I plan for the two of us to be on the road as early as possible. Hopefully she won't be in too much pain on the trip.

It can't be helped though. We need to get out of the area as soon as possible. We've already been here too long waiting for her to recover a little.

Shutting down the computer, I head into the bathroom to get a quick shower before falling asleep in the chair in the corner of the bedroom.

Chapter 3
Raven

"We need to try to leave today if you think you are up to it." Gio says after breakfast.

Instead of letting him know that I was planning to broach the same subject, I quickly agree.

"I think that's a good idea. Is there any way we can go to my apartment first?" I ask quickly.

"We really shouldn't. It's possible they have people watching your place." He looks directly at me and I wonder just how much he currently knows.

We've not yet talked about anything specific. Both avoiding having to answer the really hard questions or rather just not wanting to reveal our secrets.

There's something about Gio that tells me that whatever my wildest imagination can come up with as to who he really is doesn't come anywhere close to the truth.

"My cat. She's still at the apartment, locked inside. Please, I can't leave her behind." I beg, feeling tears prick my eyes at the thought of leaving her. She's the first pet I've ever owned.

"Fine. I'll go while you stay here though." His voice sounds harsh but I smile at him anyway.

"Thank you." My own voice filled with gratitude.

"I'll be back soon. Try to rest before I get back because even riding in a car will most likely jar you around a good bit." He says, walking out the door without my reply.

It takes a full ten minutes just as I'm about to fall asleep again that I realize he never asked me where my apartment is and I know I've never given him the address.

Just who the hell is this guy? He obviously has connections although I'm certain they are not the same connections that Scotty has.

If he were involved with Scotty or any of his men, he'd have turned me over to them by now. He definitely wouldn't be going after a cat that I almost cried over.

As soon as we get on the road, I think it's time that the two of us do quite a bit of talking. Starting with who he is and why he was in Washington D.C.

Giovanni

Since there's no way that I would be recognized, I walk straight to the apartment without any issues. I still keep a close watch around me for anything that seems out of place.

As I get to her door on the second floor, I slow down and make sure no one is in the hallway before I quietly unlock the door and walk inside, locking the door behind me.

Not seeing anything amiss as I slowly open the door, I slip inside and immediately find a cat staring up at me. It's purring loudly before it lets out a loud meow.

Taking a closer look around, I see a brand new pet crate sitting on the floor by the couch. Grabbing it, I gently pick up the feline, even scratching behind her ears before slipping her into the crate.

Thinking I might grab Raven a few clothes too, I head straight to her room.

Seeing a suitcase by the bed, I remember seeing her packing the last night I watched her from the window.

Grabbing it as well as what looks like a bag for all the shit women normally need, I grab the pet crate and head for the door.

That's when I hear someone messing with the knob as if to check if it's locked. Without missing a beat, I head to the window in the bedroom, looking out; I don't see anyone in the alley below.

Setting all the stuff on the fire escape, I climb out too. That's when I start asking myself how I'm going to get all this shit down that ladder.

Picking up the suitcase and smaller bag, I drop them over the side. If there's breakable shit in there, she'll get over it. Grabbing the crate, I go down the ladder as quickly as I can.

Once at the bottom, I pick up the two bags and never stop walking. Hopefully I got away without anyone knowing I was even there.

"All this shit for a fucking cat!" I growl and the cat lets out a loud meow.

Several hours later we are on the road. I can feel every bump as it jars my still bruised body around in the front seat.

Gio tried to make it more comfortable for me by grabbing all the extra pillows for me to sit on. I'm not sure that it's helping much but I appreciate the gesture.

I must have gotten comfortable enough to have fallen asleep because he wakes me when we get to Bedford so that I can use the restroom at a small gas station while he fills up the tank.

When I come out, he's inside the store paying for the gas so I get back in the car before anyone can see me as I am. I got a really good look at myself in the bathroom mirror. I look like absolute hell.

"Got us a few snacks to hold us over until the next stop." He hands me a bag, climbing into the driver seat.

"Where are we going anyway? I guess that's something I should have already asked." I glance his way as I pull a drink and some chips from the bag he handed me.

"Montana." He states but gives no other information.

"Is there a reason for Montana specifically?" I ask between chips.

"I have a friend that has a place where we can stay. At least until we can figure out what to do about… everything." His eyes look my way before turning back to the road.

"Can I ask you a question?" I ask. He finally nods in answer. "Why are you helping me? We don't even know each other."

He seems to think on it until I'm convinced he's not going to answer.

"I don't know." He answers and I turn back to my chips.

Several minutes later, he speaks again. "I want us to know each other though. If that's okay?" He never glances my way as if he's afraid of what I'll say. But that would be ridiculous right? This handsome as sin man afraid of what I might think.

Reaching over with my left hand, I place it on top of his. "I think I would like that." I whisper, squeezing his fingers under mine.

He seems to stiffen at first before his hand relaxes and he moves his fingers to tangle with my own. For some reason it feels way more intimate than if we were naked together.

Neither of us let go as we continue down the road in silence and I finish off my chips with only one hand.

Giovanni

Raven sleeps off and on as I continue our journey across several states. If I were by myself I would most likely drive straight through and sleep once I get there.

Finding the next rest stop along I-94, I pull in, parking in the middle of several RV's and big trucks.

"We're stopping?" She asks sleepily from the passenger seat.

"Yeah, I need to get a few hours of sleep, then we'll continue on our way." I rub my tired eyes as I lay my seat further back.

"I'm sorry you got messed up in this." She says quietly.

I look over, trying to see her in the dark but not saying anything.

"I guess I should tell you about Scotty." She sighs.

"It would be helpful." I answer.

"If I tell you, will you tell me about you? About why you were there in the first place?" She asks.

I think over my words carefully before answering her. There's quite a bit about my life that I can't share with anyone. Only my brother understands how that works.

He got lucky when he found his Fiona. But she was born into a life that has its own secrets so she never pushes him for answers that he may not be able to give.

"I'll tell you whatever I can tell you without lying. There are some things I will never be able to answer." I say.

She seems to think it over for a few minutes before she says anything else.

"I think I can work with that." She finally says. "I'm not sure where to start though."

"The beginning usually works best." I state and she snorts at me.

"Yeah, I guess it does." I can hear her eyes roll. "My parents were…are… druggies. They have been since as far back as I can remember."

She moves around in her seat as if uncomfortable. I'm not sure if it's from her injuries or from her story.

"They weren't exactly bad parents but they weren't present either. I should have left them when I turned eighteen but instead, I stayed to take care of them. They're my parents. I didn't want to know they were out on the street somewhere." She shrugs.

"When I was twenty, my dad introduced me to Scotty. He was ten years older than me and really handsome. Or at least I thought so at the time. He took me out on dates and was always super sweet to me. I trusted him. I see that was a mistake now of course."

I see her wipe her eyes as if tears are there. Not wanting to say anything that will

—

make her stop talking but wanting to comfort her, I reach for her hand. Entangling her fingers with my own.

The feeling is foreign to me as I can't remember the last time I willingly touched another person to offer comfort. I think I like the feeling though. At least with her.

"It was almost too late before I realized that he purchased me from my parents." Her admission has my entire body tightening up like a spring ready to break.

"I stayed quiet about it at first because I was always being watched. He's a rich man so it never dawned on me to ask a lot of questions about all the body guards.

But after finding out about purchasing me, I started to snoop in the files that I found in his office. I even started looking around the grounds more, especially in the places that I was told were off limits to me.

That's when I found them. The girls. The girls I was unable to save. They all lost their lives because of me." She sniffles, barely holding back her sobs.

"He did it to teach me a lesson. Told me that if I ever betrayed him, he'd do the same to me. I was so scared. It took me until the night before the wedding to that monster to get away. I can never go back. I won't!" She squares her shoulders.

Loosening myself up enough so as not to scare her with the rage I feel bubbling just under the surface, I lean closer to her, lifting my hand to her cheek gently.

"I promise, you will never go back and he will never bother you again." I whisper, trying to hide just how much I want to smash something.

She leans slowly towards me until her lips gently touch my own and I jerk back quickly.

"I'm sorry." She says, both of us staring at each other. "Thank you for being here with me." She lies back in her seat, turning towards the door.

I stay quiet, laying back in my own seat. She probably thinks I'm a freak for reacting in such a way.

Her small kiss was just a shock to me. Completely unexpected while not totally unwanted. Although she may be feeling some kind of way towards me right now since I saved her life, she may not still feel that way once she understands who I really am. What I'm capable of doing.

"We'll talk some more tomorrow." I whisper across the car but she stays silent.

——

"We should be there in about another two hours." Gio says, climbing back into the car.

We stopped yet again to refill the gas tank and to get a hamburger to quieten down my growling stomach.

"Where are you from?" I ask, popping a fry into my mouth as he pulls back out onto the road.

"I'm from a small village in Italy." He answers easily but doesn't continue beyond that.

"What's your last name?" I ask.

"Baratta."

I guess I'll only get the answer to my question without him elaborating at all.

"Any family? Siblings?" I try, yet again.

"Yes." His answer has me rolling my eyes.

"Seriously, Gio?" I huff out and he glances my way.

"I have a brother. Alessandro but everyone calls him by our last name. Baratta. You'll meet him as soon as we get to where we are going. As for other family, I have an Uncle and Aunt in New Orleans as well as a cousin." He finally says and I sigh in relief.

"What do you do for a living?" I hedge but his eyes cut over to me as he shakes his head letting me know this is something we can't talk about.

Having run out of questions for now, I sit quietly watching the scenery out my window. I can see mountains in the distance covered in snow and wonder if I'll need a heavy coat.

While he was able to grab one of my suitcases, it didn't have a lot in it as far as clothing for cooler weather.

"What's the name of the town we are going to?" I ask.

"We won't be in town but the closest one is called White Summer." He says.

Looking back out the window, I wonder why the name of a small town in Montana sounds so familiar to me? I've never been this far West before, so I know that I've never been there.

Shrugging it off, I let the quiet ride lull me back to sleep.

Chapter 4
Giovanni

It's late when we finally make it to the cabin. My brother told me he would make sure it was stocked with some supplies to get us through for a few days.

Reaching over, I nudge her arm until her eyes open, looking at me questioningly.

"We're here." I nod towards the cabin.

There's a light on so I know my brother has already started the generator ahead of us getting here. He and his wife had it wired about a year ago and mostly use it as a little get away when they can manage a weekend alone.

"You can go on inside. I'll grab everything from the car." I say, pointing her towards the door.

I watch to be sure she gets up the stairs without a problem. She's still limping a good bit but seems to be getting stronger as the days pass. The bruises may take a bit longer though.

Grabbing our bags, I follow her into the cabin. I've never been here before myself but I know that it only has one bedroom that my sister in law had added to it a year ago. The living room and kitchen are all in one room.

"I'll put your stuff in the bedroom and I'll take the couch." I say when I realize that she's noticed there's only one bed.

She smiles but doesn't comment.

"This is your brother's place?" She asks when I walk back into the room.

"It's actually my sister in laws. She had the bedroom added to it about a year ago. Said she was tired of trying to fit two people on a twin bed in a one room cabin." I answer, heading to the small fridge.

Opening it I'm thankful that my brother had it stocked before our arrival.

"Want a bottle of water? There's also some coke." I ask, turning in her direction.

"Water would be good." She answers.

Handing her a bottle, I open my own and take a drink before setting it down on the table.

"You look tired." She murmurs softly, looking right at me.

I just shake my head because I am tired. Pretty much driving straight across the country will do that to anyone. Even someone in my line of work.

"I'll go to bed too. I'm not really sleepy but I am tired. If that makes any sense." She says.

"It does. Your body is still healing." I say, staring back at her.

"Goodnight." She whispers with a smile, turning into the bedroom and shutting the door.

"Goodnight." I finally say back.

I wait for several long minutes, finishing my water before I go back out to the car quietly

---

to retrieve my other bag from the trunk of the car.

Back inside, I find the hidden latch on the floor that Alessandro told me about under the rug. Opening it, I place my bag inside, closing it again and replacing the rug.

Walking over to the couch, I lay down on it, hoping I can get a few hours of sleep. Even when exhausted I don't usually sleep for more than three or four hours at a time.

I lay there for about an hour when I hear the bedroom door slowly opening. Looking over, I see Raven standing in the door.

"Um. Do you think..that.. you could maybe sleep on the other side of the bed?" She finally asks.

My face must show my surprise to her question when she rushes on.

"It's a new place. And..I know at the other place, you slept in the chair. I would just feel safer." She says quickly, staring down at the floor.

Getting up, I walk over to her and use the tips of my fingers to lift her chin until she's looking at me. In her eyes I see fear but not fear of me.

"Okay." I whisper, following her into the room.

Getting into the bed on the other side, I lay on top of the covers while she gets under them on her side.

Facing me she says into the dark, "Thank you."

"You're welcome." I whisper back.

The next morning I wake up to the smell of breakfast cooking and noises coming from the other room.

Getting up, I move to the door and watch Giovanni as he uses an electric hot plate to scramble eggs. He looks up at me when he finishes dishing them onto two plates.

"Hungry?" He asks and I shake my head, walking over to the small table where he sets the plate in front of me.

My stomach growls with satisfaction and I see the corner of his mouth tip up.

"Thank you. It smells wonderful!" I pick up a piece of bacon and savor the taste in my mouth.

"I should have stopped more to feed you on the way here." He grumbles from his own plate.

"It was fine. I got plenty of much needed rest." I smile, trying to reassure him.

We are just finishing with breakfast when we hear a vehicle pulling up. Gio goes to the door, looking out before opening it all the way. Staying behind him, I peep from the side, unsure of who could be here.

The man that steps out of the driver side has me rubbing my eyes to be sure that I am seeing correctly.

"Twins?" My whispered word has Gio, looking back at me before he steps further out onto the porch.

"Brother." He nods to the other man who looks so much like him. "Hello, Fiona. It's nice to see you again."

I was so busy staring at his brother that I didn't notice the stunning woman covered in tattoos that got out of the passenger side.

"It's always nice to see my super handsome brother-in-law." She smiles back.

"Hey." The man next to her says back, pulling her closer. She just laughs up at him, the love she feels showing clearly on her face.

"Alessandro, Fiona, this is Raven." Gio nods my way. "Raven, this is my brother and sister in law."

Fiona smiles brightly at me. "I brought you a few things that I thought you might need while here. Gio said that you may need some warmer clothes since the weather is always iffy this time of year."

"Thank you." I answer.

"I'm going to visit with Raven for a bit. You men can bring the bags in." She points back towards the car. Neither man batting so much as an eye at her command. "Come on dear, I'll show you where everything is in case you need something. It has a root cellar but the latch is hidden." She walks right past me into the cabin, expecting me to follow.

———

Smiling towards the door, I follow her inside. She seems to be a woman completely sure of herself. Something that I'm not but really want to be. Maybe she can teach me how.

Giovanni

"I wasn't expecting you to bring Fiona with you." I say to my brother as we move further away from the cabin.

He obviously has something important to tell me considering how quickly they showed up since we just arrived late last night.

"Heard from one of my contacts that Mendez knows who you are and is tracking you down." He finally says.

"That was quick." I raise my brows.

"Yes, it was. He's got some pretty important people in his pocket apparently which means he could very well track you down through me." He looks directly at me. Telling me without words that even Fiona could be in danger.

"I'm sorry brother. I didn't know where else to take her." I explain but he holds up a hand to stop me.

"I understand more than you know. One look at my wife and I knew that I would do whatever it took to always keep her with me." He says and I shake my head knowing he speaks the truth.

"Love is kind of stupid. How can I be in love with her yet not really know her yet." I look back towards the cabin.

"You'll get to know her and that love will grow even deeper. By the time you finally tell her, she'll be in love with you too." He slaps me on the shoulder. "Look, I've talked to the President of the Wolfsbane Ridge MC. He's going to station some guys in cabins close by but there's still a chance Mendez's guys can slip by without being seen."

"Thank you brother." I say, slapping his shoulder this time.

"Come on, let's get those bags out before Fiona tries to cut out our livers or something." His comment makes me laugh. "You think I'm playing but that woman is even more volatile than ever when pregnant. I have to sleep with one eye open."

I laugh even harder all the way back to the cabin.

Raven

Gio has been fairly quiet since his brother and sister in law left this morning. I'm curious if he knows something that he doesn't want to tell me.

Fiona was super nice and nothing like I expected. She never once asked about the bruises that are still clearly visible. Instead she handed me a bottle of cream that she said was amazing and would help to heal it faster.

Fixing some coffee, I take my cup out onto the porch just to listen to the birds in the trees. I can see Gio from here chopping firewood with his sleeves rolled up on his pristine dress shirt.

It's an amazing view. The muscles in his arms ripple with each swing of the ax and I wonder what those muscles would feel like under my hands.

I stare for so long that I don't even realize he's stopped what he's doing and is staring right back at me. My face turns to fire at having been caught.

I can't help it though. The man is absolute perfection, even more so than his brother. While they may be twins, there are marked differences between them.

Gio's eyes are lighter in color and there's a very small dimple in his cheek that you'd never notice because he rarely smiles.

I continue to stare back at him, refusing to be the first to look away. There, there's that dimple as he tries to not smile at me.

He reaches down, getting an arm load of wood and walks back towards the cabin.

"I'll get us some dinner ready." He says, walking by me to go inside.

Following him, I ask, "How long do you think we'll be here?"

"It's hard to say." He shrugs. "They'll track us down eventually you know. I'm hoping to get you completely better before we have to run again."

Shaking my head, I look down at the floor.

"Shouldn't we put together a plan?" I ask.

"I have a plan." He answers, putting the wood down.

"What is it?" I ask when he doesn't continue.

He looks back up at me, his eyes going hard. "I'm going to kill them all."

Not sure of what to say to that, I ask if there's anything I can do to help with dinner. He shoos me away, so I go back to the porch step to finish my coffee and listen to the birds as the sun goes down.

Chapter 5
Giovanni

We've been here for a little more than a week. Most of her bruises have now faded and she seems more relaxed than she was before, going so far as to walk around more outside.

I've not said anything to her about staying close to the cabin, surely she knows it wouldn't be a good idea to go too far.

Scotty Mendez's men will find us eventually. I'm more than hoping that they do come. I've got some anger I need to release in some way and a few of those stupid fucks would do nicely.

Walking into the cabin, I don't see Raven at first so I head into the bedroom. What I see has my feet sprouting roots to the floor.

Raven is in a tub in the middle of the floor completely naked, washing her body. When she catches sight of me, she jumps slightly and I turn away quickly.

"Sorry." I say gruffly, striding back to the door quickly but her voice stops me.

"Gio?" She asks.

Taking a much needed deep breath trying to control the tent that is starting to pop up in my pants, I grunt back at her.

"Can you hand me the towel? I set it on the table by the door there." She says simply.

Surely she doesn't know what she's doing to me. Does she? At night before bed she puts on these tiny little shorts that when she bends over, I can see the beginning of those tight globes that would fit so nicely into my big hands.

"Gio? The towel please?" She asks again when I stand there too long.

Walking over to the table, I pick the towel up and without looking up, I walk over to the tub to hand it to her. I know the second she stands up as water splashes onto me.

Her wet hand touches my own as she takes the towel.

"Thank you." She whispers.

Unable to control myself, my eyes shoot to hers and I struggle to not look at her from head to toe. She's so fucking beautiful to me that it hurts.

Giving her a nod since I can't seem to make my throat work, I turn around quickly and stride away. Straight out the front door, not stopping until I'm far enough into the woods to breathe again.

Leaning against a tree, my cock throbs harder than it ever has before, even when I watched her get herself off back at her apartment.

That's where I stay for the next hour, getting myself back under control.

—

He's been avoiding me for quite a few days now. Ever since the evening I asked him to hand me my towel.

I couldn't seem to help myself though. Every single day I watch him chop wood, working up a sweat while his muscles ripple along his arms.

I've even started to dream about those arms and normally wake up in the middle of the night panting with my panties soaking wet. Just like I am now. Being this attracted to man has never happened to me before.

Rolling over onto my back, the sheet sliding across my skin has my nipples jumping to attention under the thin shirt I wore to bed last night.

Listening for any noises from the other room, I assume he's already outside this morning. Closing my eyes, I conjure the image of his face staring at me as I rub my own hands down my breasts to my stomach.

My core already throbbing, I push my hand into my panties, gently touching my clit. I can't stop the gasp that explodes from my mouth.

I tease my own nub slowly, building up the pressure inside while my other hand moves back to my breasts to squeeze my nipples.

My breathing escalates along with the motion of my fingers on my clit. My core tightens, letting me know it needs more but I hold off, thrumming myself even faster to that precipice.

I squirm on the bed, imagining those eyes looking up at me from between my thighs. Sliding my hand further down, I push my first two fingers as deep as I can into my slick passage.

It only takes a few pumps of my own hand and a hard squeeze to my left breast to push me over the edge.

I bite my lip to stop the scream that so badly wants out but unable to stop the deep grunt from my throat.

Breathing hard, I open my eyes, petting myself down from the high I was just on. That's when I hear a noise by the door.

Looking over at it quickly, my eyes collide with that of Gio who looks as if every muscle in his body is straining against his skin.

We stare at each other for what seems like hours but it is only a few minutes before he breaks the contact and strides out of the cabin.

That look in his eyes now has my body throbbing yet again and wanting more.

Giovanni

Swinging the ax harder than I need to, the vibrations shaking my arms all the way to my shoulders.

When I first heard the sounds that were coming from the bedroom, I knew that I should walk back out but I couldn't stop myself from walking over to that door silently.

The look on her face as she came by her own hand made me want to feel her core squeeze my cock while deep inside of her.

I've imagined taking her in so many positions in my dreams and always waking up with this throbbing need.

A few mornings ago I was dreaming of her riding me while in that tub and just as I was about to come in my dream, I woke up coming in my pants like a teenage boy without experience.

I don't have time for this. I should be on my next mission. Not dodging calls from my employers asking me just where the hell I'm at.

And certainly not panting after some woman that I barely fucking know.

But the thought of leaving her does something completely unexpected to me. It leaves my chest feeling tight as if I can't breathe.

What kind of feeling is that anyway? My brother says its love.

While I realize he fell head over heels for Fiona fairly quickly, that shit is not the norm.

Real love so very rarely happens, there's no way its hit us both.

Two twin brothers both of which are severely fucked in the head, capable of watching a man bleed out slowly without feeling anything at all.

Being with Fiona has seemed to calm Alessandro quite a bit though. As if only she can quiet the rage that is normally just under the surface, clawing to be unleashed.

Just as I'm swinging the ax again, I feel her presence behind me but I don't turn around.

"I brought you a cup of coffee. Black with sugar right?" Her sweet voice says.

Not willing to hurt her by not acknowledging her, I turn catching her eyes with mine.

She hands the cup over to me and I take it, our fingers barely touching which sends a shock up my arm.

Her eyes widen as if she felt it too, still I say nothing, putting my lips on the mug and taking a sip.

She made it perfectly, just the way I like it.

Her eyes linger on my mouth for a moment before she turns back around, taking a step away from me.

My hand reaches out before I know what I'm doing, spinning her back towards me. The motion has her front bumping into my own.

I look straight into her eyes, willing her to stop me because at this point, I can't stop myself from getting just one taste of her.

Slowly leaning down, I cover her mouth with my own. She gasps at the contact and I take full advantage, deepening the kiss.

The feeling of her against me and the taste of her mouth has my entire body turning to steel. I know at this very moment that I will never let her go. She is mine.

Raven

Our kiss was interrupted by the ringing of Gio's phone. He never said a word, just pulled it from his pocket and walked away to answer it leaving me standing there unsure if I could catch my breath. My body feels more alive now than it had earlier while thinking of him between my legs.

Turning on very shaky legs, I walk in the opposite direction, needing to calm myself before our next interaction. Otherwise I may just beg him to take me. I smile at the thought.

Walking just into the tree line, it opens up into a small clearing completely covered by early spring wildflowers. The setting is more beautiful than anything I've ever seen before.

I take a seat in the middle of all the flowers, lifting my face up to the sun, enjoying its warmth. I've never had much experience with the wilderness before, having always been in the larger cities like Miami.

Hearing leaves move in a branch, I look up to find its source. Two squirrels are playing chase across the branches and a bird close by chirps its song for all to hear.

Laying back on the ground, I close my eyes listening to the woods around me. All the birds singing their beautiful songs in the wind, relaxes me even more.

I must drift off because I wake up to Gio kneeling beside me, staring intently.

Giovanni

"What the fuck do you mean? You really want me to just hand her over to them?" I growl through the phone.

"That is what headquarters has said. Yes." Quinn says like a robot that is parroting what he was told.

I know how this works but I also know Quinn. According to the rules, I shouldn't know him but I'm a rebellious fuck. You tell me I can't and I'll do it anyway.

Quinn and I have become really good friends over the years but only so long as we can hide our acquaintance from the company.

Knowing that our conversations on this line are always monitored, I give the response that I know they want to hear but will signal to Quinn to contact me from an untraceable line.

"I understand. I'll contact you when it's done." I answer, hanging up immediately.

I pace around in a circle for nearly thirty minutes before my phone rings again. I pick it up immediately knowing that it's Quinn.

"Tell me." I order.

"The reason the FBI has yet to be able to pin anything on Mendez is because there's a certain Senator that makes everything go away. That Senator has called the higher ups in the company demanding that you hand her back to Mendez." Quinn talks quickly.

"And the Senator is?" I ask even though I know the answer.

"The same Senator that keeps the company from being shut down." He whispers.

"Wellington." I state out loud.

"Exactly. If I get anything more for you, I'll be in touch." He says, hanging up the phone.

"Fuck!" I say loudly, pinching the bridge of my nose.

This is not good. Not good at all. Needing time to think it over some more, I put my phone back into my pocket and go in search of Raven.

Going in the direction that I know she went, I find her fast asleep in the middle of a small clearing.

She looks so fucking beautiful with her dark hair spread out amongst the flowers, her face peaceful.

Kneeling beside her, I watch her sleep for a while before her eyes finally open and see me there. We stare at each other without saying a word for several long minutes.

"You look stressed." She whispers, her hand reaching up to curl along my jaw.

The touch of her hands on my face comforts me in a way that I'm not used to but don't seem to mind at all.

"We should go back to the cabin. It'll be dark soon." My voice sounding more gruff than usual.

"Okay." She answers with a smile, holding her hand out for me to help her up.

Once she's up though, she doesn't release my hand, instead she threads out fingers together with our palms touching. Pulling me slightly with our connected hands, we walk back to the cabin in silence.

Chapter 6
Raven

Ever since our moment in the clearing several days ago, I've gone out of my way to touch Giovanni in some small way throughout the day.

While he's not tried to kiss me again, I know that my plan is working. I noticed every time that I touched him before, it seemed to shock him as if he was not used to it at all.

Thinking back to when his brother and sister in law were here, they didn't touch him either. So here I am trying to gentle the beast.

After dinner, I go into the bedroom to slip on my night clothes. My usual shorts and a tank top I know always draw his eyes. It's why I keep doing it.

Going over to the wardrobe in the corner, I find the portable DVD player Fiona brought to me that first day that I charged up earlier.

Grabbing a handful of the movies, I head back into the living room area.

"Want to watch a movie?" I ask when his eyes look up at me.

"Sure." He answers, making room for me on the couch.

Instead of leaving any space between us, I sit right next to him with our legs touching.

"We can both use the blanket this way. Plus, we can see the little screen better." I say quickly, hoping he stays put.

Popping in the first movie, I set it in his lap and lean my head over onto his shoulder.

He stiffens up but I remain where I am, getting even more comfortable.

It takes him nearly the entirety of the first movie to relax, even putting his arm around my shoulders. My own hand resting on his midsection.

I soon drift off to sleep before the end credits.

Giovanni

I woke up feeling something tickling my face. Slowly opening my eyes, I'm a little shocked to see Raven staring back at me with a soft sleepy smile.

There's still only moonlight coming through the window so I know it's not yet morning time.

As I continue to look at her looking back at me, she stretches up slowly bringing our mouths closer together until she's so close I can barely feel her lips against my own.

"Kiss me Gio, please?" She whispers.

There's no way I could deny such a sweet spoken request from her.

Grabbing her waist with my hands, I drag her up closer and seal our lips together, my hands moving on their own to hold her rounded ass.

The kiss goes deeper quickly and she moans in my mouth as she grinds herself into my now hard cock. My own moan escaping from my throat.

I break our kiss but she continues to rock into me and I know from her movements I could easily get us both off while we are fully clothed.

Locking my hands on her, stopping her movements, I try to catch my breath as we are both panting like we just ran several miles.

"I'm not sure you know what you are doing, Little Bird." I whisper into the darkness.

She doesn't say anything, just reaches for my right hand, pushing it between her thighs. I can feel her wetness through her shorts and my cock throbs with need.

When I don't immediately pull away, she rocks her sweet core into my hand. Tired of holding myself back, I curl my fingers up to give her more pressure on that swollen little nub I feel.

Her hands go to the waist of my sweets, pulling them down until the head of my cock sticks out of the top.

Pulling away from me, she shimmies down my body until her mouth is just a breath away from the head. Sticking her tongue out she slowly licks the tip and my entire body nearly jumps from the couch.

"Fuck!" I yell, looking down into her face that looks entirely pleased with herself.

She does that just a few times and this will be over before it even begins. Grabbing her under her arms, I pull her back up quickly, flipping us over so she's under me.

Holding her surprised eyes with my own, I slowly lift her shirt to reveal her full breasts. My mouth waters at the sight. She reaches up, pulling her shirt the rest of the way off.

Unable to speak, I watch in fascination as she slowly rubs her own nipple between her fingers, pinching it to a point. Her pelvis rolls up into my hardness with each pinch she gives herself.

"Fuck." I breathe out.

"Yes, please." She grins back.

Getting up quickly, I jerk off all of my clothes quickly and I know the moment she fully sees my cock because she lets out a gasp.

I reach for her shorts, pulling them off quickly so that I may now see that pussy I've dreamed so much about lately.

Not giving her any notice, I latch onto her core with my mouth, sucking as hard as I can. She screams in pleasure, locking her thighs around my head.

Wanting to get her off at least once before I fuck her, I keep sucking and licking while I push two of my fingers into her wetness.

Within seconds she's coming hard, her pussy trying to squeeze my fingers but I pull them out quickly.

Grabbing her thighs, I pull her closer to my cock and thrust all the way in quickly. She yelps in surprise and I stiffen, lowering myself on top of her but not moving.

"I'm sorry. I should have been gentler." I whisper, attempting to pull back out.

"No!" She says, grabbing my hips. "You just surprised me. I want you to be you Giovanni."

"I don't think you fully understand what you are asking of me." I answer.

She stares at me for several long minutes as if truly thinking about it before her grin once again appears on her face.

"Yes. I do. Now fuck me like you mean it." She says back, surprising me.

I study her face for a moment longer before I nod back.

Grabbing her hands in one of my own above her head, I use my other arm to lift one of her legs as far as I can, opening her further for my cock to go even deeper.

I start off slowly afraid of hurting her but it's not long before her moans have pushed me to slam into her harder and faster.

The feeling of her muscles inside her let me know she's close to coming yet again.

Letting go of her hands, I lift her other leg, bringing both legs over my shoulders and her knees to her head.

I pump in and out of her quickly, her nails clawing into my back.

I'm so close that I'm almost afraid I'll explode before getting her there once more but she falls over that cliff at the same time as I do. Both of us scream out our pleasure before I collapse over her.

Once my breathing is almost back to normal, I raise up only to move her leg so that I

---

can get behind her without having to pull my cock free from inside her.

Wrapping my arms around her like steel bands, I snuggle my face into her hair until she falls asleep.

Raven

The last few days have been very different from the ones where Gio mostly avoided my company.

He even took me for a walk through the woods this morning after breakfast, holding my hand the entire way.

He still stiffens sometimes when I touch him in other ways but I'm determined that one day he won't have such a reaction, at least when I'm doing the touching.

I frown to myself because I'm acting as if he and I will still be together after all of this is over. We don't exactly know very much about each other.

"Why are you frowning?" His voice makes me jump because I didn't hear him walk up.

Looking over at him, I say, "We don't know that much about each other."

"We know enough." He says gruffly.

"No. We don't. Not really." I say.

He stares at me for several long minutes and I'm afraid he's just not going to say anything else. Instead, he sits down next to me with a sigh.

"What do you want to know?" He asks.

"Where did you grow up?" I pop off the first question that comes to mind.

"A small town in Italy. My family has a small villa there that has this huge garden with every flower you can imagine. You would love it." He looks over at me with a smile.

Looking at him closely, I realize he smiles at me more easily these days. That's progress right?

"What do you do for work?" I ask and his smile falls from his face.

"Look, I've already concluded that it has to be something that allows you to find out things that others can't and since I highly doubt it's the same type of business that Scotty is in, I'm going to say it's government related. What I'm not sure of is, what branch of government?"

We stare at each other and I refuse to be the one to look away. He knows nearly everything about me but I don't know much about him.

"Will you accept the answer that it's top secret and that I'm unable to share anything about it with you?" He asks with a seriousness that sets off alarm bells.

"You can't even tell me if it's the FBI or something?" I ask.

"I can't let you know anything Raven. Your life, hell, both our lives depend on it." His eyes go hard and I know deep down that he means exactly what he's saying.

My thoughts though do not quieten down.

What part of our government could get away with such a thing?

One that's not officially listed, that's for sure.

Giovanni

She will never know how very much I wanted to be able to share everything with her. Hopefully one day I can do so without worrying that the company will send others to take her out. Others like me.

Those of us that can look through a scope, put one through the eye of someone and walk away without feeling anything at all.

That's why I've been taking the time to hunt down the location of someone that I know is in a position to help. A position with more political pull than Senator Wellington.

And I have something he'll want. Something he'll pay whatever price I set to keep it from getting out.

But it's also something the company will be coming for. Soon. I'm surprised they haven't already.

It's actually been too quiet from them lately which means they are already on the move. I just need to keep my eyes open at all times.

My first priority is to keep her safe, even if it costs me my own life. It's time we moved locations.

I've been too distracted lately, letting the feel of her in my arms relax my natural senses.

Walking back towards the cabin determined to pack up and move tonight, something starts to not feel exactly right.

Slowing down, I take my time scanning the area around the cabin for any signs of something that shouldn't be there.

That's when my eyes zero in on a shadow against a tree on the far side. I quickly move behind the tree next to me, pulling my gun from behind my back.

I don't see Raven anywhere and wonder if she's inside already, completely oblivious to what is about to happen outside. I can only pray that they don't already have her.

I'm about to move to another spot to get a better shot when something sharp jabs into my arm. Looking down, I see a dart sticking out.

"Fuck!" I say out loud. Within seconds, my vision is blurring before my body hits the ground.

I can just make out a figure of a man before my entire world goes dark.

Chapter 7
Raven

Giovanni went outside a while ago and hasn't come back yet. Deciding to do the dishes before he returns, I run water into the sink.

I'm almost finished when I look out the window and spot him coming through the trees. I'm about to yell out the window to him when I see him fall to his knees.

My eyes widen at the sight but I stay quiet knowing something is wrong. Moving quickly over to the small pantry in the wall, I open the door then kneel down trying to quickly find where Fiona showed me to open the false bottom in case of emergencies.

Hearing a step on the porch, my finger finally finds the hidden latch and I pull it open quietly, I go down the small stairs softly pulling the latch closed above my head.

There's not much room down here so it doesn't take much feeling around to find the flashlight that Fiona said was at the bottom.

Turning it on, I see the tunnel that she said to head down. Taking a deep breath, I crawl through hoping that she is right and that it will not cave down on top of my head.

I get tired eventually but not wanting to take the risk that someone found the entrance behind me, I push on.

After a little longer, I think I finally see light shining in and hurry in that direction.

Stopping at the end, I slowly look out into the trees to be sure no one is out there before I climb out and head towards the river.

Fiona told me that once I make it to the river to keep straight across the fields until I come to a huge house with a barn. She said to ask for Hayden. That she would get in touch with Fiona.

Finally hearing the sound of water, I run faster, crossing the river quickly. I'm out of breath by the time I see a big barn and a house in the distance.

Making it around the barn, the people walking around pause at seeing me but I ignore them determined to get to the house.

Stepping up to the door, a man wearing a leather vest comes out of the door with a frown.

"Can I help you?" He asks, not moving from in front of the door.

"I need to speak to Hayden." I say between gasping breaths.

"I'm Hayden." A woman pokes her head out the door.

"Fiona said to only talk to you." I look at her, not sure of the guy still blocking my path.

She seems to push him completely out of the way although with his size, I'm completely sure he let her.

"Blood, can you call your sister please? I'm going to take our friend here to wash up and get a cold drink of water." She smiles at him, putting her arm around me and walking us inside.

As we are walking through the door I swear I hear the man she called Blood murmur something about these damn women.

"But." I try to turn back towards the door, unsure if I should say anything to these people about Gio.

Leading me into a bedroom, she leaves me in the middle of the room as she walks over to the closet and starts pulling out clean clothes.

"I think these will fit you. There's a bathroom right over there. Clean towels and other toiletries are in the cabinet." She smiles in my direction.

"Don't you want to know who I even am?" I look at her with confusion.

"Your name is Raven and you have been staying in the cabin with Baratta's brother, Gio."

"No one was supposed to know we were there." I say in a rush.

"They don't. We women of the club know how to keep secrets." She grins.

"What club?" I ask, confused yet again.

"The Wolfsbane Ridge MC. You walked right past some of the guys on your way in here."

"The ones with the vests?" I ask and she shakes her head.

"Go ahead and get a shower to clean up. You can meet us in the kitchen when you are ready. Fiona will be here by then."

"Thank you." I say before she leaves through the door with a smile.

Catching a glimpse of myself in the mirror on the wall, I realize the reason some of them stopped short when they saw me walking across the yard. I look like a monster that was buried alive.

Turning the water on, I strip down to get into the shower. I pray that Gio is still alive.

I find my way to the kitchen without any issue at all by following the voices of women. Turning into the doorway, I spot Fiona on the other side of the room.

She cuts off from speaking as her eyes find my own. I run to her as she wraps her arms around me and I burst into tears on her shoulder.

Although we don't know each other all that well, I feel more connected to her than anyone else in the room currently. She's the only face that I really know here.

"Shh, you're okay now." She says in a soothing almost motherly voice. "Baratta will be here in a few minutes and then you can tell us everything, okay?" I just shake my head, still unable to let go of her.

"Prez is on his way." I hear a deep voice and I stiffen but Fiona doesn't let me go.

"Go back outside! You're scaring her!" Fiona growls at the man.

"How the fuck can I be scaring her? She's not even seen me?" The man sounds almost like he's whining.

Wanting to get a peep at him, I let go of Fiona slightly and turn towards him. A large man with huge muscles is frowning at Fiona.

"Just go back outside!" She snarls and I hear him mumble something about all these crazy ass women as he stomps to the front door. Exactly like a toddler probably would.

The whole thing is just funny to me and within moments I'm laughing so hard, tears are streaming down my face once again.

All the ladies in the room join in too.

"I can't believe you talked to him like that. He's a big guy!" I finally say.

Fiona shrugs her shoulders, looking back at the door he left from.

"I can still kick his ass!" She yells loud enough for him to still hear her outside.

"While these men around here look like they could snap any of us in half, they really are just big teddy bears. They'd never do anything to hurt us." Hayden says from the stool she's sitting on at the small bar in the middle of the room.

"Come on, let's all get a drink and go sit under the tree. The biggest two asses will be here soon and will want all the details." Fiona grabs enough beers from the fridge and leads the way outside.

All of us follow her lead with our heads held high right through the middle of all the huge ass men standing on the porch.

Giovanni

Waking up to a mostly dark room, I keep my breathing even so as not to alert anyone that I'm awake.

I take everything in at once. My hands chained above my head to a wall. Chains also attached to my ankles so that there's barely any movement on my part.

Letting my eyes adjust to the darkness, I search the corners for Raven in case she was taken as well but the room is empty.

My eyes are just getting used to the darkness when I'm blinded by the door opening and the lights overhead coming on.

"About time you woke up." A slick haired man comments as he moves further into the room with what I assume are his bodyguards. No way would this asshole get his own hands dirty.

Looking him over swiftly, I can tell he's used to money with how he wears that ridiculously expensive suit. Not that I don't have some of those myself.

"Mind telling me where the girl is?" His question gives me the only real answer that I wanted. They don't have Raven.

The next question in my head though has me questioning the loyalty of those that I work for.

"Mind telling me how you found me?" I grin when his mouth forms a firm line.

He's not used to being questioned back. This could be fun.

"You'll answer eventually. The only question will be how badly you'll suffer first." He curls his nose looking over at his goons.

"Get the information that I want before you kill him." He says, walking back to the door.

"Might as well kill me. You'll not get the information that you seek." I murmur quietly.

"Yes. They said you would be a hard one to crack. But we will. Crack you that is. We'll split your head wide open and you'll give me what I want." He snarls.

Standing as tall as I can with my shoulders back, I smile at him.

"Give it your best shot." I laugh out when he stomps his foot like a child, storming from the room.

His men start in my direction and I just smile wider.

"Let's play, shall we?" I'm almost giddy with excitement at the prospect.

These fucks have no idea just how much I love pain. They may make me bleed, but I'll love every fucking minute of it.

Chapter 8
Raven

When Baratta finally got here, I broke down yet again.

He looks so much like his brother that everything just hit me like a ton of bricks.

When they were able to calm me down once more, I told them everything I could remember about the men that were at the cabin.

Baratta and the President of the Wolfsbane Ridge MC assured me that Giovanni would still be alive as the guys that showed up obviously were after me.

The real question is, how did they find us?

"You need to stop worrying." Fiona says from her seat next to me and I just smile back at her.

The girls and I are all still sitting under the shade tree with our drinks. I've barely touched mine.

All the men went inside after speaking to me to discuss what they needed to do next.

I wanted to listen in as well but was told to stay out here with the other girls.

We all hear what sounds like Baratta yelling and we all turn our heads towards the house just as he slams out of the door.

He begins pacing, rubbing the back of his neck as he does so.

"Shouldn't you go to him?" I ask Fiona, once again worried about what's going on.

"Nope." She pops the P in the word. "That's his pissed face. I ain't getting in that." She sits back, drinking her beer. She keeps her eyes on him though.

"They must have found out something." Miranda, one of the girls I met this afternoon, comments and the other girls shake their heads in agreement.

"Must not be a good thing." I whisper, still looking back at the house as Miranda's husband walks out to talk to Baratta.

A few minutes later, a car races up the drive, throwing rocks as it goes. The driver almost slams on brakes, skidding to a stop just behind a few of the bikes.

It must be someone they all know, as not even the guys on the porch react to the crazy driving.

A small petite woman hops out of the driver's side, gives the men on the porch a one finger salute and walks our way.

I watch as she stomps over muttering to herself before she plops down into a chair next to Bella who just smiles and hands her a beer.

"So what's happening?" She demands.

"Raven, I'd like you to meet our Queen B around here. This is Mina. She's the Prez's wife." Fiona introduces her.

She nods her head in my direction but waits for someone to answer her question.

I leave the explanations to the other girls as I zone everything out again. I feel so tired that I lay my head back on the chair, closing my eyes.

I must have fallen asleep because the next time I open my eyes, Fiona is shaking me gently.

"Come on. Let's get you in a room so you can rest."

Letting her help me up from the chair, she leads me inside the house and into the first room we come to.

I don't even take time to look around as she tucks me under the covers and turns out the lights.

I'm asleep once again before she ever walks out the door.

I watch my men as they look over the footage that Snake is able to send back to us of the building that these assholes have Giovanni in.

They didn't take him very far, just on the other side of Billings so it wasn't hard to find them.

He wasn't able to tap into any surveillance that may have been at the property, so he launched one of his high tech drones that has infrared cameras.

While it can only show us the bodies that are moving around inside, we can still see one in particular that never moves around the room.

That has to be Giovanni.

"Looks like there are only five guys total besides Gio. Should be easy in and out." Bear says, looking up from the computer on the table.

"Do you think Mendez is still there?" I ask, looking at Baratta.

"No. My contacts say he's a smart man. He'd have left his goons to do his dirty work. He's most likely back in Miami waiting for them to bring Raven to him."

"They'll come after them again." Blood states the obvious.

"Yes. But I know my brother. He won't sit back and wait for them this time." Looking back at Blood with a serious expression. "I'll be going with him."

Blood looks over at me and I already know what he's asking without him saying a word. He'll be going as well.

Rubbing my temple that is already starting to throb just from the thought of having to deal with Fiona's shit over all of this, I just nod back at him.

Blood and Fiona are club family so by extension Baratta as well as Giovanni are as well.

"Let's go get him from this hell hole first, then we'll deal with what we need to do next. And just so you fucks know, you both can be the one to tell Fiona that you'll be gone."

They both chuckle back at me but Fiona has been more moody since getting pregnant. There's already been a few times when she has busted out into tears without notice then mad as hell the next.

I understand hormones and shit. I went through that with Mina but Fiona has been worse in my opinion.

"Get the men ready. We're leaving in fifteen minutes." I tell Blade who walks out to round everyone up.

Walking back into the kitchen, I find Mina sitting with the other girls except for Raven.

"Where's the girl?" I ask, walking up kissing the top of her head.

"She was worn out. Fiona put her in the room just down the hall." She answers and I nod my head.

"You guys must be heading out soon." Miranda states.

"Yeah. We'll be back as soon as we can." I look down into Mina's eyes.

While I can't promise anything even though there's only five men at the location we are headed to, I try to assure her with my eyes that everything will be okay.

Leaving her behind to wait for me for things such as this will always hurt. I'd hate to not be able to make it back to her but this is the life we live.

I'll wait to tell her I'm going with them to Miami. No need to make her pissed at me just yet.

Giovanni

"Just tell us where the fuck she is!" The man screams for the hundredth time through my laughter.

Blood is pouring from my face that is swelling with each new blow. The pain doesn't bother me like it should.

The way normal people should feel pain.

I'm not normal though. Neither is my brother.

We've known that since we were small boys. Our family, what's left of it, knew it too but loved us anyway.

They taught us a different way to deal with not being what others consider normal.

A phone ringing blares through the room and I try to stop my laughing long enough to hear the stupid fucks answer it.

"No, Boss. He's not talked yet."

He's quiet as his boss screams over the line. I know he's screaming as even I can hear him although I haven't a clue of what he's saying.

"No matter what we do, he just keeps fucking laughing!" The idiot who's been hitting me for the last couple of hours says.

"I'll get it done!" He finally says a few minutes later before hanging up.

"What'd he say?" One of the others asks from the door.

"What the fuck do you think he said?" He growls back. "Hand me the whip." His mouth curls up, looking right at me but I just smile back as best I can.

There's no way they could know about my demons.

My father used to beat me with a whip that had razor blades on the ends, then stick me in a closet. He only ever opened that door to pour gas on my open wounds.

I watch as idiot number one turns back to me with a whip in his hand.

I hold his gaze, not letting him know the fear that tries to bubble up remembering my father.

Just as he gets behind me, we all hear an explosion that rocks the whole building.

As the men in the room run towards the sound, I grin widely knowing that Baratta is now in the building.

Hopefully he saves one just for me to play with.

"Fuck, man!" Blood coughs as he tries to fan the dust from in front of his face.

"What? Think it's too much?" I smile over at him. "We needed to get their attention."

Gunfire explodes through the door. The stupid fucks can't see us for all the dust my explosion stirred up.

Blood and I don't move from our positions on opposite sides of the door frame.

I'm counting on these guys to be stupid as evidenced by the fact they didn't station anyone to watch the door.

As the dust settles, I hold my finger up to Blood to make sure he stays as still as possible.

Just as I predicted, a barrel of a gun slowly emerges out the door.

Waiting just a second longer, I grab the gunman, jerking him outside at the same time that Blood shoots towards the other idiots inside.

Breaking the wrist of the one I grabbed, I quickly take his gun apart and turn back to the door leaving the guy yelling about his wrists on the ground for one of the other bikers to tend to.

Just inside the door, I slowly scan the area, not seeing the rest of the crew left behind with my brother.

"There's three more." I whisper to Blood.

"I'll take this way." Blood nods to the hall on our right, leaving me with the hall on the left.

The one that should lead straight to the room where Giovanni is being kept.

Timber and the rest of his men have the place surrounded in case anyone decides to try to escape.

There's no escape from this, they will all die this day.

Just as I'm passing one door, the corner of my eye catches a small glint of metal from a slightly open door further down the hall.

I duck just as a bullet hits the wall behind where my head was.

Just as quickly, I pull my own trigger and hear a thump as a body hits the floor. A few minutes later, I hear other shots from further away.

"I got two." Blood says in my ear piece.

"With the one I got, that should be all of them." I say back.

I still don't let down my guard as I make my way towards a room in the back, looking for my brother.

Opening the door slowly, I see Giovanni strung up in the middle of the room.

"Took you long enough." He says over his shoulder.

Shrugging, I walk over, untying him from his position.

"Did you save me one?" He looks over at me.

—

"The one outside should still be alive." I answer.

His whole face lights up with a grin that probably looks sinister as hell to most people considering the blood that's all over his face.

"Did you find him?" Timber asks through my earpiece.

"Yes. Can you bring in the asshole I left outside?" I ask back.

"Absolutely." Timber laughs.

A few minutes later, Timber along with a few of his men dragging in the first idiot whose wrists I broke.

"Oh, this is going to be great!" Gio grins down at the terror filled face of the man.

I watch as he walks over to a table filled with all kinds of things that I assume they were using or going to use on him.

My eyes widen as he picks up a whip that has razors attached to long strips of leather designed to rip the skin to shreds.

Looking up at Gio, I wonder if he still has nightmares about what our father did to him.

He's never said anything to me about it since we have gotten older but something inside of me tells me he does.

"We'll be outside brother." I turn towards the other men and motion for them to follow me outside, leaving Gio to do what he must to settle his own demands.

Before we make it to the door, the man receiving my brother's wrath screams out in pain.

Chapter 9
Raven

I pace back and forth on the front porch watching the long driveway for any signs the guys are back.

The other girls all got a text about an hour ago that they had found Giovanni and would be heading back soon.

Looking down at my watch, I sigh once again and continue my pacing.

"They'll be here soon. You should sit down before you fall down." Mina says from the porch swing.

"Shouldn't they be here by now?" I huff, knowing that I sound almost childish.

"They should be here any minute." Fiona says.

"You said that twenty minutes ago!"

All the girls laugh at me and just as I am getting even more annoyed, we hear bikes rumbling closer in the distance.

As they come into view, my eyes zero in on the jeep. The windows are too tinted for me to see inside.

I wait for them to come to a stop before I fly off the porch in their direction.

Getting to the jeep just as Gio climbs out of the passenger side, I skid to a halt scanning his face that is covered in blood and swelling.

"Looks worse than it is." He says breaking my stare.

Finally throwing myself into his arms, he hugs me tightly to his chest.

"I'm okay little bird." He pulls back, looking into my eyes with a grin, that's all him.

"I was so worried." I whisper, tears clouding my eyes.

"How about a shower brother and something to eat?" Hayden asks from the porch.

Giovanni pulls away but laces his fingers through my own as we all make our way inside.

We excuse ourselves to the room I was in earlier so that Gio can use the shower.

I sit on the bed as the water turns on and I want nothing more than to go in there with him.

There's a quick knock on the bedroom door that makes me jump and I roll my eyes at myself as I open it.

"We figured he could use some clean clothes." Fiona holds out her offering with a smile.

"Thank you." I say as she nods, walking away.

Shutting the door back, I walk towards the bathroom and slowly open the door.

"Just bringing you some clean clothes." I say over the sounds of the shower.

Trying my best to not look, I set the clothes on the counter and turn back to the door just as the shower curtain is pulled open.

"Come here little bird." His growl pulls my eyes in his direction.

Standing there with water splashing everywhere, he's a sight to see.

He's muscled everywhere, even his thighs that look thick enough to kill a man with one kick to the head.

My eyes taking him in fully, my bottom lip gripped between my teeth, I watch as his manhood grows stiff.

"Come here." He growls even lower and my feet move without me telling them to.

I stop right in front of him, looking up into his eyes.

"Strip." He commands and I do as I'm told while holding his gaze.

Once every piece of clothing is gone, he continues to stare at me before raking his eyes over every inch of me.

I feel my body heat along with his gaze, my nipples becoming stiff points begging for attention at the same time my core gushes with wetness.

His arm snakes out and I gasp as he hauls me into the shower, pulling the curtain closed.

Steam rises from the hot water, my body heating even more.

"This will be fast and hard." His voice is strained and I whimper.

Bringing his hand up, he holds my chin, looking into my eyes.

"Are you afraid?" He asks and I shake my head.

"Say it out loud little bird."

"I'm not afraid."

His mouth slams down on my own, kissing me more deeply than I've ever been kissed.

Moaning into his mouth, I feel his hands on my ass just as he lifts me in the air and I wrap my legs around his waist.

He pushes into me, using the wall at my back to help hold me up, he hooks his forearms under my thighs spreading me further, lining his cock up with my entrance.

Pulling back, he looks into my eyes as he slams into me in one full thrust.

He pulls back, slamming into me again over and over like a jackhammer while holding my gaze.

My eyes flutter from the sensations he's creating inside of me and one hand comes back to my throat gaining my attention.

"Eyes on me." He growls but doesn't release my throat although he doesn't squeeze.

It's so erotic. Him commanding me to hold his gaze, his hand at my throat and his cock hitting places inside me that's never been hit before that I'm sent into an orgasm quickly.

As my pussy throbs, squeezing his cock, he groans out his own release.

Hot liquid squirting my insides just as I remember that he wasn't wearing a condom.

Drying off and quickly getting dressed I sit on the bed to wait for Gio. It takes him longer because of his injuries.

As soon as he steps out of the bathroom I pounce. "Who was that? How did they find us?" Not stopping I continue, "Are they after you or me? Who are these people?"

"We'll talk later, Okay? Everyone is waiting for us in the kitchen." He sighs.

Giving in, I walk back to the kitchen with him and make our plates before sitting down with everyone else.

No one really talked about what happened at the warehouse where they found him which I found very odd.

All the men were laughing together about an incident with one of them and the pile of horse manure from the barn. Even the women joined in, acting as if this was just like any other day.

After eating the women all got up to help clean up. I wanted to go with Gio and ask questions but I didn't want to be rude.

Once the kitchen was clean again, I searched him out but didn't find him outside with the other men.

Going back to the room we are sharing, I finally hear his voice as I get closer but it sounds as if he's talking to someone on speaker phone although the voice doesn't sound exactly right.

Trying to keep my footsteps as quiet as I can, I lean towards the door trying to listen without getting caught.

"The company can not sanction this." The other voice says.

"You can tell the company that I don't give a fuck." Gio growls.

"You're not going to let this go." It was more a statement than a question.

"No." His voice is clipped.

"She has become an obsession for you. She's a liability." My heart skips that they are talking about me.

Gio says nothing to refute the statement.

"If you want me to continue, you'll give me what I want and I'll give you what you want." He finally says.

After a few quiet moments, the voice says. "We will be in touch."

I stand there wondering what all of this is really about, my mind thinking furiously. When the door jerks open suddenly, I squeak in surprise.

"You shouldn't listen in on others' conversations." He says sternly.

Pushing my way into the room, I spin around with a glare.

"You want to tell me what the hell that was about?"

Giovanni

I swear Raven is going to pass out if she doesn't take a breath between questions that she isn't even giving me a chance to answer.

Everything happened so fast she's probably in shock now that the adrenaline is wearing off.

"One…two…three…" I count

"Why the hell are you counting?" she shouts at me.

"Count with me. One… two…three." I repeat.

She looks at me as if I've lost my mind but she gives in. As she counts with me I can visibly see the tension leaving her body.

Finally after repeating the count a few times, she sags back on the edge of the bed.

"You need to calm down. I'll answer the questions that I can but I can't answer everything."

"Calm down? You did not just tell me to calm down!" she jumps back up.

Oh shit, as long as Fiona has been my sister I should know better than to tell a woman to calm down.

Instead of putting my foot any further in my mouth I just pull her into my arms and hold her until her breathing is back to normal.

"I can tell you that those men were after you, not me." I finally say with a sigh.

"Who were you just talking to?" She looks up at me.

Thinking over what to say, I settle on the truth although it's only a half truth.

"The people I work for." Her eyes narrow at my face.

"That's it? You're not going to elaborate? Who do you work for?" She pushes away, demanding.

"I can't tell you that."

Jumping up from the bed she starts pacing and I just watch her. The way her body moves naturally seems to call to me in a way that I'm not used to.

My handler was right. She's an obsession and a liability but I'm not willing to let her go.

She stops every few minutes, looking over at me before her pacing starts yet again as well as mumbling that I can't decipher.

"So let me get this straight." She pinches the spot between her eyes. "You work for someone that you can't tell me who they are. Therefore I guess it's top secret making it a government entity?"

"Not exactly." I answer softly and she rolls her eyes.

"You're making this difficult." She sighs, sitting down next to me once more.

"I'm sorry. If I could tell you, I would. I would never lie to you but there are some things about my job that I will never be able to tell you."

"Let's move on. The guys that took you. What happened to them? Did they get away?"

More tricky questions from my little bird. I have to be careful here as well because even the MC has strict rules about keeping secrets within the club.

Raven nor I are part of that club even though my brother is married to one of the club members' sisters.

"They did not get away." I answer, holding her stare, expecting her to ask the inevitable question of what happened to them.

Instead she just stares back for a full minute before lowering her eyes.

"What now?" She asks and I take a relieved breath that she's willing to drop it. At least for now.

"Now? Now I go after the man himself. Mendez." Her eyes pop back up to my own.

"How are you going to do that? He could kill you." She asks, breathing hard as her heart rate kicks up.

Reaching over, I cup her face into my hands.

"I need you to trust me when I tell you that I will do whatever it takes to keep you safe for the rest of my life."

"Trusting you isn't the issue, Gio. The issue is how long that life is going to be." She answers with tears in her eyes.

Smiling back at her, I bring her face closer to my own. "No worries little bird, that life is going to be a long one as I'm going to need every minute of it to explore this obsession that I've had of you since I first laid eyes on you."

Taking her lips with mine, I kiss her deeply until she relaxes once again into my arms.

Chapter 10
Giovanni

It took several days to hear back from my handler with the news that I had been waiting for. Even if they hadn't called back, I was still going after Mendez.

A man like that would never stop coming for what he believes to be his. Even a woman that is adamant about not wanting him back.

Several of the guys from the MC are going with us. Judging from the looks a few of them are getting from their women, if they don't make it back alive, the women will bring them back to life just to kill them themselves.

I tried to talk them out of coming along but Timber was dead set on going. He informed me that I was considered part of the club family just for being Baratta's brother.

This will be a new experience for me. To have others with me on a mission. While I'm sure that would normally bother me, I'm grateful for the help on this one.

Mateo "Scotty" Mendez is basically behind a fortress that is protected with some of the highest levels of security a man in his position can buy.

Throwing my bags into the SUV along with the other stuff, I turn back to the house where Timber is currently telling Mina goodbye.

Raven walks out of the house and holds my gaze as she comes towards me.

Wrapping my arms around her, I pull her close and breathe in her sweet scent just behind her ear.

"You'll be careful?" She mumbles into my chest.

"Of course."

Pulling back, she looks at me with a serious expression.

"You come back to me!"

Not answering, I pull her back into my arms and kiss her thoroughly.

I will never make her a promise that I can't keep and while I plan to come back to her, it's not a promise that I can make.

A few minutes later we head out. Looking out the back glass, I watch her figure as it gets smaller the further we get from the house until I can't see her any more.

The look on the face of the guy at the airport is hilarious when a bunch of motorcycles pull up to his door.

My brother keeps his private plane here but he doesn't often have anyone with him except his wife.

We spend the flight going over plans and contingencies.

One of my contacts was able to find us blueprints of Mendez's compound and another contact had a schedule of guard rotations. I didn't ask either of them how they got that information.

Just when I think this would be easier as a one man show, my brother points to something on the blueprint.

"What's this?" Baratta asks.

Taking a closer look I see what looks like a tunnel. After flipping through all the documents in front of me I realize it's an underground escape route that leads to the beach in an area blocked off to the public and it doesn't seem to be guarded except through electronic surveillance.

If I had more time I could hack into it, but I don't want to give anyone a chance to discover we are there.

I start to dismiss it, when Timber suggests he can have it hacked and under our control before the plane even lands.

"Brother," I call out expecting Baratta to answer.

But when the club members answer instead he just grins at me. How the hell did I suddenly obtain all these brothers? Looking each man in the eye, I just shake my head.

"I meant Baratta." I laugh. "I don't dare call in anyone else, I don't know who I can trust. You got any local connections to arm us?"

"Yeah. Think I know someone."

By the time we land, we have transportation, weapons and a plan.

Jeramiah

Getting a call from Baratta for a favor that I still owe him was a huge surprise. After sending him the coordinates of where to meet me, I borrowed a boat from a certain gentleman that won't be needing it any time soon.

I spot him and his men as soon as they get to the dock. Scanning their faces, the only one I recognize is his brother, Giovanni who spots me immediately and says something to his brother.

Jumping down to the dock from the boat, I walk towards them, meeting them in the middle.

"Jay." Giovanni says and I nod back.

"Did you get what I requested?" Baratta asks straight to the point.

"Everything is already on board." I nod towards the boat.

Looking over at it, his smile surprises me as I've only ever known him and his brother to be blank of all emotion. Never showing a single weakness regardless of the situation.

Giovanni finally makes the introductions to the other men with them before we haul their gear onto the vessel and pull away from the dock.

As I steer the boat, the men gather around the computer that is currently hacked into the surveillance footage of the tunnel that leads into the Mendez compound.

"It's been recording since I hacked into it. We just need to make it play the recording back to their live feed so that they never see you coming."

"You did great, Jay. Thank you."

I nod acknowledgement as I slow the boat, stopping far enough away that the camera's to the entrance can't see.

"That's it." I point and all the men stand to look in that direction.

Turning away, I kneel down to the trunks I brought on board, opening them all to reveal the weapons and gear.

"Jesus, where'd you get all this?" The one named Timber asks, kneeling to pull out a machine gun.

Shrugging my shoulders, I smile widely. "It came with the boat."

"Untraceable?" Giovanni asks.

"More like if anything is found after, it'll trace back to the cartel. No worries. I know what I'm doing." I narrow my eyes.

"Didn't mean to imply otherwise." He states.

"How exactly do you three know each other?" Timber asks.

Smiling over at him, I answer, "They trained me."

"You should have just let me kill him." Giovanni growls to his brother who just shakes his head.

"If I had let you do that, then he wouldn't be here helping us now."

Giovanni just grunts, turning his own attention back to the equipment.

"Let's get strapped up. It'll be dark soon."

I look towards the setting sun and once again for the thousandth time this past year, I feel a heaviness that I've never felt before and I rub my chest just above my heart.

"Are you doing okay?" Giovanni asks next to me. "Quinn said that something with you has been off lately."

Squaring my shoulders, my eyes still on the sun set, I reply, "I'm fine."

Taking my answer as is, although I get the feeling he doesn't believe me, he walks back to the other men preparing for what's to come.

I didn't exactly lie to him. I am fine, it's just that lately I've been feeling like something is coming. I just need to figure out if it's a bad thing.

Giovanni

Slowly and quietly, we make our way through the tunnel toward the compound. According to the map, it leads straight to a trap door in the kitchen of the mansion which we all thought was odd.

The blueprints of the place show that the kitchen is a recent addition that also happens to be the only part of the house that is not connected to the basement.

Remembering some of the things that Raven told me, Jay, Timber and Blood are to check the basement. My brother and I will make our way to the main quarters where Mendez should be.

The plan is not to take out everyone inside the house as we are very much out gunned. Just Mendez. I want him dead for what he's done to my Little Bird.

As we make our way up the stairs barely avoiding a few heavily armed men, I hear a few grunts through my earpiece.

"Two down in the basement." Jay whispers over the line.

A few minutes later we hear Timber's voice. "Holy fuck."

"What is it?" Baratta asks as we hide in the shadows assessing the two guards outside the door leading to Mendez's room.

"There's a few girls down here. One in really bad shape."

"Can you get them back to the boat?" I ask quietly.

"The one won't make it. We'll get the others." Jay answers instead and I know it must be really bad if he's willing to leave one behind.

"Get the girls back to the boat. We are almost to Mendez's room. We'll be right behind you."

Looking over at my brother, I nod my head and we both take aim at the guards, shooting at the same time using silencers.

The bodies fall immediately and move to the door, slowly opening it to look inside. Not seeing another guard, we pull the bodies inside and shut the door silently.

Hearing grunts coming from the bedroom, I peep through the slightly open door.

Mendez is laying on the bed as a woman is on top riding him. Her face is blank of all expression as she rides his dick and he rubs on her tits.

Preparing to go in, Mendez pops up, putting the woman under him and starts slamming inside of her quickly until he roars out his release.

Finally done, he pulls his limp dick out and with a curl to his lips, demands she clean up the mess from his bed. He pulls on a robe and walks out the doors leading to a balcony.

The girl in question pulls all the sheets from the bed and walks into the bathroom.

Moving quickly, I grab her, covering her mouth and indicate that she should be quiet.

Eyes wide with fear, she shakes her head and I remove my hand.

"I'm not going to hurt you. I need you to stay right here with my brother." I nod to Baratta who walks up behind me. "We'll get you out of here."

Still not speaking she nods her head as tears gather in her eyes.

"Take her. I've got this."

Moving over to the door, I look out to be sure that Mendez is alone. Scanning the outside area, I spot several men on the roof across the yard.

Keeping my eyes on them, I wait until they are all turned away before I reach out and hit Mendez hard enough that he falls. Grabbing him, I pull him inside, shutting the balcony doors and pulling the shades closed.

"What the hell? Who the fuck are you?" He groans, holding his now bleeding head.

"I have a message for you. From Raven."

At the mention of her name, his lip curls up.

"And what message might that be? Where is that fucking bitch anyway?"

Not saying a word to him, I grab my knife from my side, slamming it down into his heart as I cover his screaming mouth with my other hand.

He tries to fight. His arms come up to hit me in the face but he's too weak.

Leaning down to his ear, I whisper, "Have fun in hell."

Twisting the knife quickly, he gives out one last grunt before the light fades from his eyes.

Wiping the blood from my weapon, I stand up and make my way back to the door. Baratta; having already taken the girl back out the way that we came.

These fuckers always think they are so smart. Untouchable. They've just never come face to face with me.

I'm the real monster in the shadows. The one you never see coming.

Chapter 11
Raven

Gio and I have been staying in one of the guest cabins since they all got back from Florida a little more than a month ago.

I've tried to broach the subject as to what's next for us. Our relationship. If you can even call it that. I'm not exactly sure what we have.

He's had to take several trips that were business related that he refused to tell me anything about. Some more of that top secret shit he keeps swearing he can't tell me about. So he's not been here in White Summer for more than a few days.

This trip he's been gone for a week already. At least he did find a moment of his time to text me late last night to let me know he'd be a few more days.

I quickly texted him back but I've still not received anything else from him which is pissing me off.

Swinging the door open to the cafe, I walk in, taking a deep breath of the wonderful food smells that permeate the air and make my stomach growl.

The last day or two I've felt a little queasy throughout the day suspecting that I'm catching the flu or something.

Taking a seat, I pick up the menu and scan it quickly to make a selection.

"Hey! What brings you into town?" Looking up, I see Bella standing next to my table with a smile.

"Food. I feel like I'm starving today." I say but before she can say anything back, my stomach growls loudly and she laughs.

Giving her my order, I sit back to wait for my food. Picking up my phone that Giovanni gave to me, I open up our text messages but there's of course still nothing from him. With a sigh, I slam the phone back down.

"I wonder who's face you were thinking of just then." I hear laughter in Fiona's voice as I look up.

"He sucks at texting back!" I growl as she takes a seat.

"Most men do." She shrugs. "What did you want to talk about?"

"I think I'm gonna go back to D.C." I state as Bella arrives with my food.

"Hold that thought." Fiona holds a finger up to me. "Bells, can you bring me a cup of tea please?"

Bella, taking the hint that even I noticed, nods once and heads back to the kitchen.

"Why the hell do you want to go back there?" She demands.

"I have a job there waiting for me. I liked it there."

"What about Giovanni?" She looks at me a little confused.

"What about him?" I demand back, taking a big bite of my food that seems to really hit the spot.

Not bothering to look up, I pretty much scarf my food down as if I've not eaten in months.

"I think you might want to slow down there before you make yourself sick." Fiona's comment has me looking up from my food.

"Sorry. I've not been feeling exactly right the last few days." Grabbing my water, I take a few sips.

As I'm sitting it back down, my stomach seems to swirl and the powerful urge to vomit hits the back of my throat. My eyes catch hold on Fiona who's own eyes widen. Jumping up from the table, I make a run for the restroom. Making it just in time.

As I'm leaning over the toilet, one hand holding me up, I feel a cool cloth being pushed into my hand.

"Thought you'd need this." Bella says softly.

Standing back up, I wipe my face with the cloth before turning around to face both Fiona who has her arms crossed and a smile on her face as well as Bella who just looks sympathetic.

"Before running off to D.C., I think a trip to the doctor is in order." Fiona raises her brows at me and all I can do is close my eyes.

If this winds up being what I suspect, will Giovanni even want it? I wonder to myself.

I don't even know if he wants me for the long term. We've not had time to have those serious conversations.

Looking back at the girls, I ask, "Is it a walk in clinic?"

"Come on. We'll take you to get this test, then we'll talk about what to do about my brother in law." She smiles as we move towards the door.

Giovanni

I had called my brother to check in with him around lunch only to find out that Fiona had Raven at the doctor's office.

I asked repeatedly if Raven was okay and he said she had just been feeling under the weather the last few days. That everything would be fine.

It didn't feel fine in my gut though so I wrapped up my business and got back to my brothers' private plane at the airport as soon as I could.

A few hours later, we are landing just outside of White Summer.

"I told you she was fine." Baratta mumbles as I step off the plane.

"I was ready to come back anyway." I shrug, throwing my bag into his jeep and climbing in. "Where is she?"

"Back at the cabin now. Fiona dropped her off about an hour ago."

"She told you what happened at the doctor?" I demand.

"No." He's quiet for a second longer than he should have been. Anyone else wouldn't have noticed but since I'm his twin, I know him well enough to know that he's lying.

I stare hard at him until he looks at me out of the corner of his eye.

"It's her business to tell." He growls low.

Knowing that he's right and afraid that it's something really bad, I sigh deeply but sit back in my seat quietly thinking as we make our way back to Wolf's Landing.

Pulling up to the cabin, I can make out Raven's shadow through the window and climb out of the jeep, grabbing my bag.

Baratta pulls out of the driveway before I even get to the porch steps. I can hear music inside which must be why Raven didn't come to the door when we pulled up.

Opening the door, the music is even louder and I walk further inside in search of her. Leaving my bag by the couch, I walk towards the kitchen and see her at the stove swaying to the music.

"You don't look sick." I say loudly over the music.

She jumps at the sound of my voice, the spoon in her hand flying through the air and landing on the floor.

"Jesus! Don't sneak up on me like that!" She growls back before her face softens. "Who told you I was sick?"

"My brother mentioned that Fiona took you to the doctor. That you haven't felt very well for several days." I walk towards her slowly, looking over her features carefully and noting that she does look paler than usual.

"I'm fine. I didn't know you were coming back today." She looks away.

Stepping close enough to touch her, I turn her face back to my own.

"I thought you were sick." I explain.

"That's why you're here? You thought I was sick?" Her brows come together in a confused expression.

I nod my answer as I glide my fingertips across the soft skin of her arms. I'm fascinated by the goosebumps that spread across the skin that I've touched. My mind wonders if I can make the rest of her body do that with my tongue.

"What are you smiling at?" She asks.

My eyes on hers, I grab her around the waste and haul her up to me.

"Why were you at the doctor?" I whisper in her ear as I kiss the side of her neck.

"Um…" She sighs in my arms.

"Are you going to answer me, my Little Bird?" I smile against her skin but she pushes me away, putting distance between us.

"I'm going back to D.C." She squares her shoulders.

Confused about where she's going with this, I shrug.

"Okay. We'll pack tomorrow but we are not staying in that hovel you were in before."

I step towards her again but she backs up a step.

"What do you mean we?" She makes me look up at her and it dawns on me that she has no idea that she has me completely and forever. Unless she's not wanting me.

"You don't want me going with you?" I cross my own arms.

"Answer my question, Gio. What do you mean we? Who are we? Are we in a relationship? In a friendship with benefits? What are we?" She almost yells the last bit.

Stepping forward, I pull her to me, locking my arms around her.

"We are all of it. You and me. How could you not know that? You had me before I ever found you in that alley."

She looks deep into my eyes and I want her to see exactly how I feel about her. Reaching on her tiptoes, she takes my lips with her own.

My hands slide down her ass, pulling her further into me. Feeling a piece of paper sticking out of her back pocket, I pull it out. Feeling what I did, she breaks the kiss and tries to grab it but it's too late.

I already see exactly what it is although it currently only looks like a tiny bean or blob in the picture.

Looking back at her, I see that she's holding her breath, waiting to see what I'll say.

"We most definitely are not staying in that hovel!" I announce with a grin and she laughs.

"So you do want us?" Looking into her face, I watch as a tear rolls down her cheek.

"How could you think I wouldn't?" I ask.

"I don't know." She shrugs. "You've barely spent any time with me or even acknowledged me in a text while you were gone."

Pulling her even closer, I lay my face into the top of her head.

"I'm not used to having someone that needs me. I'll do better." I promise, holding her tightly.

"I'm not sure if I can handle not knowing where you are or what you're doing either." She pulls back, looking at me with honesty in her eyes.

"I'll share with you only what I am allowed to share with you. You have to know that it's for your own protection. You have to trust in me."

"Trusting you isn't the problem. I already know you'll keep me safe. Keep us safe." She rubs her stomach lightly. "What if something happens to you?"

"Nothings going to happen to me. I'm one of the best at what I do."

She rolls her eyes at me. "Which is something I can't know about. I do however know it's dangerous as hell. You can't deny that!"

"No. I can't but I will always come home to you."

She sighs deeply, laying her forehead into my chest once more.

"We'll see if I can learn to live with it." She says a minute later.

Holding the sonogram in my hands, I vow that I will always keep them both safe with me.

Chapter 12
Jeramiah

Throwing back the shot, I slam the glass back down in front of me and wait for the bartender to fill it once more.

Something's been off with me for months and my handler decided that I was too distracted so the Company has yet to reassign me a month later.

Throwing some money down on the bar to cover my tab, I grab my phone and walk back to the hotel that I'm currently staying in.

Locking the door behind me, I strip off my clothes on the way to the shower.

Just before turning on the water, I hear my computer signal that I have a new message.

Walking over to it, I open the encrypted email. Seems the Company has decided that a month's vacation is long enough.

Opening the files attached, I scan over it quickly. It's a top secret mission that will require going into deep cover South of the border.

Shutting the computer, I walk into the shower and cut the water on. Stepping into the cold spray.

It'll be good to get back into the action. Back to work, doing what I do best.

This mission is for Intel only. They are hoping to take down the head of the cartel.

Not that I think it'll do much good.

Soon as you take one out, another takes over. It's a never ending cycle that is usually connected to those who are supposed to help end the drug crisis.

Whatever. I'll get my part of the job done. The rest is up to someone higher up the ladder than me.

Milena

I've been awake for several hours now. Sleeping on this concrete floor every night is taking its toll on my body.

I'm already bruised from where the men here knock us around if we don't do as they say. They mainly use us to get drugs across the border into the U.S.

Some, though, get used in other ways. So far I've been lucky on that part.

If I ever make it out of here, the first thing I'm going to do is kill that asshole that put me here.

My step-father, the bastard as I like to call him, never really liked me but there was nothing he could do about me while my mother was alive.

I knew that as soon as she passed away, that I would need to leave. I just didn't know that I should have left before the funeral instead of after.

He'd tried to accost me one night after I got home from work while mom was asleep.

The pills the doctors had her on didn't help her much other than making her tired all the time.

She slept through the whole thing and I didn't have the heart to tell her about it. I'm sure she knew it was coming though.

She even told me that as soon as my schooling was done, that we would both leave.

So I went off to school but by the time I came back she was so bad off there was nothing I could do to get her away from him.

We didn't have any money to pay for the doctors on our own and certainly couldn't afford a place. We would have had to leave the area anyway as he would have found us.

Hearing the men coming to wake us up, I open my eyes and look towards the door at the end of the hall just as a man I've never seen before follows one of our jailers into the cell areas.

His face never twitches but there's something about his eyes that just tells me he's angry. About what, I'm not sure. Maybe they skimped on his drug order.

As they pass by the chain link area that I'm in, his eyes catch my own long enough for chills to pass down my spine.

Death is in those eyes. Dark and sparkling, they hold my gaze until I finally look away.

"Damn, he was sexy." One of the other girls' comments.

"You're out of luck Lucinda! His eyes were totally on the new girl." Another says.

Looking over at them in the fence next to mine, the first one that spoke curls her lip at me.

She's one of the ones that gets special treatment around here because she spreads her legs for the men any time they want it.

"Don't mind me, you can have them all!" I growl, turning my back to them all.

No way in hell I'll willingly spread my legs for these nasty fuckers. I don't give a shit how sexy they are.

Thank you for reading Giovanni's Obsession. Watch for Jeramiah and Milena's story, Coming Soon!

Continue to the following pages for a sneak peak at Torque's Gaze Available NOW!

**Torque's Gaze
Wolfsbane Ridge MC Series
Book 6**

**Chapter 1
Torque**

Walking around the reception, I watch my brother Bear smile more than I've ever known him to do so. I'm happy for them but the whole falling in love bit isn't for me.

"Another wedding, another brother, leg shackled for life." I shake my head.

"One of these days some woman is going to come around and change your mind about love." Blade says from beside me.

"Of course you believe that, you're one of those that got leg shackled." I laugh. "Women, especially the ones that come into this club, are fucking crazy." I growl.

"Still sore about the snakes, huh?" He laughs.

"I'm still planning my revenge. I got to wait for Fiona to pop out my nephew first though. Then it is on." I vow but Blade laughs even more.

Before I can call him what I'm thinking of calling him, a tiny hand grabs my arm.

"Hey Uncle T!" I look down at Luna, Prez and Mina's little girl. She holds her arms up to me indicating she wants me to pick her up which I do and set her on the table between Blade and I.

"Shouldn't you be playing with the other kids?" I ask.

"I was trying to build a castle in the sand box but Hunter knocked it down and told me I wasn't a princess." She pokes her little lip out.

"Of course you're a princess!" I argue for her and get a cute little grin. "Come on, I'll help you build a bigger one."

Lifting her from the table, I nod at Blade as Luna and I walk towards the huge sandbox the Prez had built for the kids.

That's where I stay until the parents of the kids order them all to bed. Then I proceed to drink as much as possible, making it back to my room and passing out some time around three in the morning.

I wake to a cold nose pressed against my own. Opening one eye slightly, I'm met with a low playful growl from my dog Titan.

Titan was a street dog. I adopted him when he pissed on my buddy Austin's ex-wife. After treating him to a steak dinner, he hasn't left my side. I'm thinking about getting him his own sidecar and goggles so he can ride with me.

I don't even have to look at the clock because he wakes me up every single day at the same time, exactly like today since I took him off the streets.

"One of these days you're going to sleep in and I'm going to wake your ass up." I murmur to him.

He sits back on his haunches, tilting his head to look at me. When I close my eyes for longer than he likes, he yips right in my ear.

"Fine! I'm getting up!" I rise up on the bed just as he jumps around in circles, moving closer to the door.

Putting my clothes on quickly, as well as my boots, I grab my shades from the night stand, slipping them on before grabbing his leash.

"Let's go see if Bella's Brew has those muffins we like so much." I say, opening the door. He barks back in answer, more than ready for breakfast.

We take my jeep into town, parking right in front of the door. You can smell the coffee and other baked goods from outside.

Walking in with Titan at my side, more than a couple of the people inside, move around us, not wanting to get close.

I guess Titan does look more than a little scary. He's a huge ass dog with a wide head that's a credit to his breed. But it's also that breed that everyone is so afraid of without even having a reason to be so. Kind of the way most are afraid of bikers.

We get in line behind everyone else waiting to place their order. I'm looking towards the back, hoping to get Bella's attention when someone runs into my back.

"Oh, I'm sorry. Excuse me." I hear a very feminine voice.

"That's okay." I answer automatically.

Looking at the woman, I'm shocked at how beautiful she is. Her heart shaped face looks up to me for only a minute before looking down at Titan who has pushed his whole face into her midsection.

"Hello handsome guy." Her voice didn't have that sweetness in it for me. Hell, she's actually barely acknowledged me. This never happens. Women always turn back for another look, even with my shades on.

She's not the classic beauty that I see so many men chase after. She's short, her head barely coming to my chest with rich dark hair, dark eyes and plenty of meat on her bones.

I really love those kinds of women. The ones that I don't feel as though I'll break if I put my arms around them.

Still not looking at me with any interest at all, she smiles slightly in my direction before walking out the door.

"Oh, did you meet the new veterinarian? She's such a sweet woman." Bella must have come up next to me when I was distracted.

"That's the new town vet?" I ask, looking back at the door.

"Yep. You'll probably see her a good bit over at Hayden's place for a while. They are still trying to find what's making the horses sick. Here, I saw the two of you out here, figured I'd bring you the usual. We are super busy this morning." Bella says in a rush.

"Thanks." I reply. "Think I'll take this to the park and let Titan play for a bit while we eat." I say.

Leaving Bella's Brew, I think back on the beautiful Veterinarian. I hope I do get to see more of her. With a smile, I enjoy my breakfast just a little more than usual.

Jesse

Sitting at my desk, I read through every page the state agricultural lab sent back on all the samples that I collected from Wolf's Landing, the Dude ranch owned by the local motorcycle club.

When I first opened my new veterinarian clinic in town, I wondered about the guys in leather that I would see riding their bikes.

None of the townspeople seemed the least bit concerned with them which helped to put my mind at ease. Where I'm from, men on bikes and dressed in leather should be avoided at all costs.

It seems that their club is very welcome in this town although when I did some digging on the internet about them, not everything that popped up was pleasant to read.

I met their Vice President, Blade, first at the local coffee shop. Since then, I've met quite a few more while working out at the ranch for Hayden. Several of her horses have gotten sick from some type of toxin that I've yet to find after testing nearly every plant and water source on the property.

Whatever the toxin is, it's gone from their bodies quickly without a trace. That in itself has me worried that someone may actually be injecting the horses directly with something.

From what Hayden has told me though, the only ones working out there are directly connected to the Club.

She's adamant that it wouldn't be one of the brothers. I'll take her word for it. I certainly don't want to point fingers. Several of them look as though they could easily bury me alive and sleep like a baby that same night.

"Did they find anything?" Remy, my assistant, asks, walking in behind me.

"Nothing." I sigh, tossing the papers down.

"What now?" She asks.

"Now? Now we wait. I asked Hayden to keep the horses in the pastures they have been in. Hopefully we can figure out which pasture is being targeted." I answer.

"So we're waiting for another horse to get sick?" She asks with concern.

Shaking my head, "Yeah. It sucks but at this point it's all we can do. I'll still go out there and take a look around every chance I get. I'd rather not watch another horse die like that."

"Me either." She answers softly. Hearing the bell above the door, she heads back towards the reception desk.

Grabbing my lab coat, I get ready to see my next patient who's coming in to get her stitches out after having her leg amputated.

Three legged cats can do everything a four legged one can. Hopefully, this time, she

___

stays away from the highway if she gets out again.

My feet are killing me a few hours later as I walk around the clinic locking up. My stomach rumbles reminding me that I skipped lunch again today.

I've still not gone to the grocery store and decide that I'm not going to tonight either. It's just easier to pick something up from Bella's Brew.

Of course my sister, Annie, wouldn't approve. She thinks I need to be on a diet. According to her, I'm overweight.

And what if I am? I like my curves exactly where they are. It's better than looking like the stick my sister resembles.

My phone rings as soon as I get to my car. Figures it would be her as if I conjured her with my thoughts.

Getting into the car, I let the phone connect before answering.

"What took you so long?" She demands before I can even say hello.

"I'm just now getting into my car." I roll my eyes. "What's up?"

"We went to the same school; can you at least try to speak properly?" She huffs. "Mom would be so disappointed to hear you right now."

"Good thing you're not mom then." I smile towards the phone.

"She says you're not answering her calls."

"I've just been busy. Besides, she just wants to berate me for starting my practice way out here in the sticks as she put it."

"Well she does have a point Jesse. You could make so much more money here in the city."

"That's not what I wanted. All of you knew that the whole time I was in school. I told you both multiple times I was finding a rural town to start up in. One where I could work with farm animals as well as house pets. You both should be happy for me." I roll my eyes.

Remembering that I have a candy bar in my center console, I dig it out. She must hear the paper as I tear it open.

"Not sticking to your diet then?" She asks.

"I don't need to be on a diet. Besides, I missed lunch today."

I hear her sigh through the phone gearing up for the argument that always ensues.

"You're never going to catch a good man if you don't take better care of yourself."

"First of all sis, I don't need a man when I have a vibrator that doesn't talk back unless I flip his switch. Second, I can take care of myself. Now, I've gotta go find something for dinner and head home."

———

"God, you are so crude!" She sighs again. "I still love you though." She says quietly after a short pause.

I stare at the phone and wonder what has gotten into her. She rarely tells me that.

"I love you too. Are you okay?"

"I've never been better. Go home, get some rest. We'll talk later." She hangs up quickly.

Shaking my head, I put the car in gear and pull out of the parking lot. She wouldn't tell me if anything is wrong anyway. She'd be afraid of me saying I told you so regardless of what it is.

I think she's wrong about me never finding someone though. One day there will be a man that will love me just the way I am. All my extra curves included.

Bulging muscles and tattoos would be a plus for him. I can just see my mother's face when seeing one of her daughters with such a man. That would be the highlight of my life.

A few minutes later the smell of Bella's Brew takes over my senses as soon as I walk through the door causing my stomach to rumble with happiness.

"Hey Jesse! Have a good day at work?" Bella asks as soon as she sees me.

"Let's just say it was a long day. My feet are killing me and I'm starving!" I smile, taking a seat at the counter.

"You've come to the right place. Do you need a menu or do you want the special of the day?" She points to the sign.

Lasagna is the special and already has my mouth watering at the thought.

"The special will be just fine."

"Coming right up!" She smiles but turns towards the door opening up.

Her smile widens even more as she watches her husband walk through. The love they hold for one another is clear for all to see with how they look at each other.

"Evening Miss Jesse." Blade smiles my way once he lets go of his wife.

"Good evening." It tickles me with how well mannered he always is with me. It just doesn't seem to fit him if you judge by the leather he wears.

My food arrives soon and I tackle it like a woman that hasn't eaten in months. I can't help it. I love food, especially food that takes over all your senses the way Bella's does.

"Good wasn't it?" I hear Blade from beside me.

"I'm sorry. I missed lunch today." I feel my face flame with embarrassment.

Throwing his hands up, "Hey, I'm not judging. I eat it the same way!" He points down at his empty plate.

"What does she put in her food anyway? I swear it's become my drug of choice since moving here." I laugh.

"It's a secret recipe. As they all are." Bella answers, walking up to the counter.

"You certainly found your calling." Gathering up my purse, I begin to dig out my wallet to pay my bill before heading home.

"We're having a cookout out at the Wolfsbane Clubhouse Saturday. You should come." Bella says.

"Aren't those for club members?" I raise my brows.

"Not this one. We have one a month out there that the entire town is invited to. Quite a few usually show up, especially the ones with kids because Mina always gets those inflatable water slides and things for the little ones to play on." Blade answers.

"Just say you'll be there. You can meet everyone else." Bella says.

"Sure. I'll be there. It's not like I have any plans anyway." I shrug with a smile.

"Awesome! We'll see you then!" Bella bounces on her heels excitedly. There's no wonder most call her a Pixie. She certainly looks like one with how tiny she is.

Getting back to my car, I head home and to my bed.

Pulling up at the clubhouse on Saturday, I can see there are a lot of people here already.

Kids are running around everywhere wearing swimsuits and shooting each other with water guns.

Walking around to where everyone is at, I scan the crowd for Bella and Hayden. We all spot each other at the same time and they wave me over.

"You made it!" Bella says.

"I was beginning to wonder if I was going to be able to find a parking spot. There's a lot of people here." I laugh, taking a seat with the girls.

"I'm working on that. I've already mentioned to Timber we need to expand on the parking." Mina smiles over at me.

"Bet that went over well!" Hayden laughs.

"He informed me that if everyone would ride a bike, there would be plenty of parking and no need to expand." She shrugs.

"He does have a point." Another woman who seems to be extremely pregnant in the group says.

"Oh, Jesse this is Fiona. She's Blood's sister and also the owner of the tattoo shop, Poison Pen in town." Bella introduces us.

"When are you due?" I ask her.

"Any fucking day and I can't wait!" She sighs dramatically.

"She's currently a day over her due date." Mina says. "I've already told her she should walk around. It could help."

Fiona narrows her eyes at her. "And, I've already told you I look like a fucking whale trying to move around on land!"

They all start arguing with each other about how to help Fiona go into labor soon. "You know sex can induce labor." I flippantly say while looking around. I notice the kids playing in the sandbox and spot the guy I ran into at Bella's Brew earlier in the week.

The women break out laughing when Fiona replies, "No uh, no way that's what got me in this condition."

When I first saw him I pretended that I barely noticed him when really, I felt my woman bits scream for attention. I've yet to even see his full face since he was wearing shades indoors. The same ones he's currently wearing.

He has a huge smile on his face as a beautiful little girl attempts to cover his boots in sand. I'm so busy watching them in the sandbox that I jump when a wet tongue licks my hands.

Looking down I see a beautiful huge pit bull begging for attention. The same one that was with the sexy ass biker at Bella's Brew.

"Hey beautiful boy." I smile, rubbing his ears.

"That's Titan. He belongs to Torque." Bella says from beside me.

"Torque?" I raise my brow.

"The guy you've been staring at this whole time with the sunglasses." Fiona announces loudly.

I feel my face flush red.

"Jesus, Fi. Don't embarrass her just yet. We might want to keep her around!" Mina throws a wadded up napkin at her when she just shrugs.

"She might as well get used to me now." She groans, pushing her hand to her side.

"You okay?" Hayden asks as we all scoot to the edge of our seats.

Fiona waves a hand to all of us. "Baby just kicking my side really hard."

We all sigh in relief.

Torque

I noticed her as soon as she got here. Watching as she made her way over to the other girls. The woman is sexy as sin. When I noticed a few of the guys noticing her, I felt something I don't usually feel about a woman. Jealous.

I keep my eyes on her even while playing with the kids in the sand. Mostly just to be sure no other fucker talks to her. For some reason, I've decided she is mine. For how long remains to be seen. Right now, I'd settle for just tonight.

When I notice Titan head directly for her and demand attention I hide my smile as best that I can. That's right boy, soften her up for me.

I stay away during the bar-b-que not yet wanting to go up to her. Another first for me, I normally like to get it over with. Something tells me I need to move slowly with this one.

"Seems your dog has made a new friend." Prez says taking a seat next to me at the table.

"A beautiful one too." Blood adds, taking the other seat.

"I hadn't noticed." I shrug playing it off.

"Liar!" Blood laughs. "I'm surprised you've not moved in for the kill. Could it be that this one doesn't seem to notice that you even exist?"

"I've noticed that as well." Prez agrees.

"Could you two just fuck off?"

They both laugh at that suggestion.

A few hours later when the party is winding down, I watch as she leaves saying goodbye to the girls.

Right before she heads around the building she looks back, our gazes colliding even through my shades. I grin in her direction and watch as her face turns the perfect shade of red.

I wonder if she turns that color all over. Fuck! I gotta find out that answer. Adjusting myself, I whistle for Titan and head towards my jeep ignoring all the pussy clearly on offer. I don't want anyone else but Jesse to calm this ache. No one else will do.

Get It NOW:
https://books2read.com/TorquesGaze

About the Author

Marissa Ann spends her time in rural North Mississippi with her husband, the kids and all of their animals on a hobby farm.

She always said she would write books one day even though many thought she never would. She made a promise to a childhood friend who left this world for the next in 2015. That she would finally write and publish at least one.

Her first book hit the market in 2018 and she's never looked back. She now has several out with many more scheduled for release. Want to stay up to date with new releases, giveaways and all the cool things?

Sign up for Marissa's newsletter here and get a free short story prequel to Reaper's Jewels: https://www.authormarissaann.com/

Or join **Marissa Ann Romance Readers** on Facebook.

List of Marissa Ann's Books

Timber's Fairy
Blade's Pixie
Blood's Angel
Wrench's Salvation
Bear's Saviour
Torque's Gaze
Fang's Miracle
Reaper's Jewels
Grease
Buzz
Skeeter
Giovanni's Obsession
All I've Got
Baratta's Darkness
Lily's Shadow
Arin's Light
Mika's Heart
Cass' Vow
Shelby's Secret